THE WAY HOME

The Wobbly Wallaby III

MIKE SKILLICORN

Published by Skill Creative in 2019
Cover Design by Nieves Barreto
Instagram: @nievesbarretoart

ISBN-13: 978-0-9945088-5-0

www.thewobblywallaby.com

For Wally.

...and for Bongo.

CONTENTS

I'M WALLY

Peg set a cracking pace along a trail that led across the ridge and back down to the river beyond the waterfall. Although the path was wide across the ridge, it narrowed as it descended, and soon the wallabies were travelling in single file. It quickly became obvious that the Rocky Hill wallabies weren't used to travelling at such speed, and Peg soon found herself well ahead of the group. She turned to hurry them along.

"Come on, you lot!" she cried. "We haven't got all day!"

"Oh, what's the rush, Peg?" called Jake, who was more than happy with the relaxed pace of the Rocky Hill wallabies. "We've got a long way to go. Can't we just take it easy for a while?"

"What's the matter, Jake, can't keep up?"

"It's not just the four of us anymore. There's no need to go like a bull at a gate."

"Fine. I'll take a breather if someone else wants to take the lead."

"I'll do it," replied the big male from the Rocky Hill mob, taking the opportunity to slow things down. He'd been struggling to keep up with Peg and was already breathing heavily.

Peg stepped aside and let him through.

"You're Peg, aren't you?" he asked.

"That's right."

"Good to meet you, Peg. I'm Ned. You three seem a lot fitter than we are. It's been a while since we've travelled this far or this fast," he said. "It might take us a little while to get back into shape. We're used to spending most of our time just lying in the sun." He flashed her a smile as he moved to the front and started down the trail.

Peg fell in behind him. "Come on now, not too slow, or we'll be on this trail forever."

Wally had been travelling towards the rear of the group and found his mind wandering as the trees flashed by, his thoughts drifting to Gus, stirred by his words and the memory of his passing. He tried to fathom how the dingo could have crossed the Divide. There was no way he could have climbed the boulders, and he was too small to have made the jump across the Leap. Not only that, he'd figured it out quickly, so he must have been clever. He was probably only a day or so behind the wallabies the whole time, and it occurred to Wally that things could have turned out a lot differently.

They'd let their guard down since crossing

the Divide, assuming the dingoes were stranded on the other side. Maybe if they hadn't been so preoccupied with crossing the river, that dingo may have snuck up and taken one of them in their sleep. And if one of the pack had crossed the Divide, what about the other two? Were they still stalking them?

A dark thought flashed through Wally's mind. "I should have killed that dingo while I had the chance."

Just then, as his mind drifted into darkness, his knee misfired again. There were no acrobatics this time; he simply flew sideways into the bush and tumbled down the hill, narrowly missing a thick tree. The two Rocky Hill wallabies behind him stopped at once.

"Are you alright?"

"Yeah, I'm fine," Wally muttered, his irritation masking his embarrassment. His knee had been working so well until the fight at the rock pit.

"What happened? One minute you were hopping along, then suddenly you shot off into the scrub. Did you trip on a rock or something?"

"There was no rock. I've got a tricky knee. It's been behaving itself lately, especially with all the distance we've covered, but I twisted it during the fight with Doogan. Now the misfires are back."

"Misfires?"

"Every now and then, without warning, my

knee does something odd and I go careening off in some random direction. Strangely enough, hopping seems to be the only thing that fixes it. It'll get better, I'm sure."

"Is that what happened when you flew over those guards at the rock pit? We all heard about that."

"Yep."

"So it's not always a bad thing."

"No, but I can't control it. That's the problem."

"I thought you had an unusual jump," she smiled. "Like you've got a pebble in your paw or something."

"I know, I know."

Wally picked himself up, dusted himself off, and hopped back over to the trail.

"Come on. We'd better catch the others," he said. "We don't want them getting too far ahead. I'm Wally, by the way."

"Hi, I'm Wiru, and this is Ellin. Why don't you go first, in case you have another misfire?"

"I'll be fine," said Wally. "You don't need to worry. I've come this far with this knee, I'm sure I can get to the end of the day with it. Ladies first," he added, extending a paw toward the trail.

As Ellin and Wiru hopped past, Wiru smiled. "Thank you, sir."

Wally watched them hop away for a moment before following. Travelling last would at least save him the embarrassment if it happened again.

It took the rest of the day for the wallabies to find a passage through the bush that would lead them back down to the water. The thick scrub had slowed them down, but they finally emerged onto the stony bank of the river. Tired and thirsty, they were all happy to stop for the day. After a long drink, they retreated into the cover of the bush.

"That was a long day," said Ned, collapsing onto a patch of grassy mulch.

"You're not kidding," replied another of the Rocky Hill wallabies. "I'm beat."

"I think we all are," said Wally. "Hopefully it'll be a bit easier tomorrow. That bush was pretty thick." He scratched a couple of burrs out of his fur. "By the way, we never really introduced ourselves. I'm Wally. This is Jake and Peg. I've met Wiru and Ellin..."

"I'm Ned."

"And I'm Agnes. This is my son, Banjo," Agnes added, pointing to her joey. "He's only three months old."

Not wanting to be left out, Darcy piped up. "And I'm Darcy. I'm Peg's joey."

"You're not my joey, you silly thing!" said Peg, laughing. "Darcy gets a free ride in my pouch. He sleeps most of the day," she explained.

Darcy blushed.

Wally noticed the curious looks from the Rocky Hill wallabies. "We went through a fire before we got to the Divide. Darcy lost his home. He's been with us ever since."

"So you really did come through the Divide?" asked Ellin.

"Yes. A couple of eagles chased Peg and me up the boulders," Jake said as he settled down. "Wally took the easy way and jumped across the Leap."

"The easy way. Very funny."

"Why, what's at the Leap?" asked Agnes. "I've never actually been to the Divide."

"The Divide is a huge stone wall that separates the dry, barren land to the west from the land on this side," Jake explained. "There are only two ways through. You either throw yourself at a gigantic wall of huge boulders and bounce your way up, hoping you don't get stuck while eagles try to tear you apart. If you don't make it all the way up, you're stranded on the stones with an almost impossible job of getting back down."

"Or you jump across the Leap," said Wally. "The Leap is at the end of a massive ramp. You have to leap over a huge chasm and land on a tiny ledge on the other side. The ledge is below the ramp, so you're already falling when you hit it."

"Oh, you two can talk it up!" said Peg. She turned to the Rocky Hill wallabies. "I won't say it was easy, but one way or another we made it through. Honestly, the scariest part was following Wally into the dingo ambush."

"Who's talking it up now?" Wally countered, smiling at her.

"A dingo ambush?" asked Agnes.

"Yes. Four dingoes were waiting for us at the Divide, hiding in the bush. They had been tracking us ever since we left our mob. There were originally five dingoes, but one got taken by the crocodile..."

The Rocky Hill wallabies' eyes widened at the mention of a crocodile, and that was all the prompting Jake needed. He picked up the thread of the story and wove it into a rich tale full of danger and suspense, stretching the truth as far as Wally and Peg would let him. His retelling of the encounters with the crocodile, the dingoes, and the river grew larger and more fearsome as he went on, while the trauma of his infected tail barely got a mention. By the time he finished, Peg was laughing.

"Now tell them about the journey the three of *us* went on," she said, laughing through her words. "You can really lay it on thick, Jake!"

"It's all true!" Jake insisted. "Every word!"

Peg turned to the Rocky Hill wallabies. "What about you? How did you all end up at Rocky Hill?"

"We didn't have much choice once the dogs

arrived," Ned began. "They came into the mountains in large packs and terrorised us."

"When you say dogs, you mean dingoes, right?" asked Wally.

"No, they weren't dingoes. Like a dingo, I suppose, but much bigger, and there was a lot of them. They came out of nowhere and devastated our mob. So we left the mountains and came across the Rocky Hill mob. They let us stay with them. It was a much smaller mob then, and the dogs hadn't discovered Rocky Hill, so we felt safe. But over time, the remnants of more and more mobs, all victims of the dogs, started to arrive at Rocky Hill. The commander grew less accommodating as time went on. When the dogs finally found us, everyone was too scared to leave. Now the dogs come back almost every month."

Ned paused at the memory of the dogs.

"Then you three came through and shook things up. I have to say you didn't look too healthy when you arrived, but to take on Doogan at the pit? That was the push we needed to get us moving."

"Doogan," Wally muttered, the thought of the big wallaby and the intentions of the mob turning his mood. "He was a nasty piece of work."

"He used to be our commander before we got to Rocky Hill. He was a good leader once. But the Rocky Hill commander saw how useful a wallaby his size could be, so he was invited into their inner circle. It wasn't long after that he started to change."

"Well, it's ancient history now," said Jake, keen to lift the mood. "I think we did pretty well today, getting through all that scrub and back down to the river. Looks like the landscape flattens out from here, so it should be easier going tomorrow."

"I hope so," said Ellin. "I'm exhausted. It's been a long time since I've travelled that far in a day."

The rest of the Rocky Hill wallabies echoed her words, and the little mob began to settle in for the night.

Sleep took them all quickly that night, with barely a whisper of resistance. All except for Wally. He rolled over and thought again of Doogan. Enemies could be anywhere, even where you least expected them.

LOST

"Oh, for heaven's sake," said Horatio. "What happened to 'Bongo the Brave', or whatever you were calling yourself? More like 'Bongo the Cry-baby', if you ask me."

"Well, no one's asking you," replied Bongo. "Alright, I had a moment. A bloke can have a moment every now and then, can't he?"

"A moment?" said Horatio, shaking his head. "Your whole life is a moment. One long, crazy moment. One minute you nearly kill me on the bridge and the next minute you're having a little 'moment'."

Bongo just grunted.

"Come on then, dry your eyes and let's get moving. That river looks like just the place for a long drink and a well-earned swim. We've been walking in this heat for so long, I reckon if you shaved my back, I'd have a tan."

The two devils made their way through the bush and, after bickering almost the entire way, finally arrived at the bank of the river, a short distance upstream from where the wallabies had stopped. There was no hesitation when they saw the water; they both ran straight in without any thought of danger, Horatio up to his neck, and Bongo content to roll around in the shallows.

"Ahhh, that's better," Horatio said, as the cool water soaked his fur and cooled his skin. He stood completely still, bracing himself against the current, letting the water flow around him, swirling through his legs and toes.

He turned and looked at Bongo just as he stood and shook the water from his fur.

"Hey look, you're black again."

Bongo looked down at his fur, now clean of the reddish-brown dust he had been carrying for the last few weeks. "Look at that," he said, proudly admiring his coat. "I feel positively Tasmanian again!"

Horatio dunked his head and shook it, knowing that his shiny black coat would be clean of dust too. To Horatio, it felt as though they were washing off a terrible chapter of their journey and starting afresh. The land was fertile, they had found a seemingly endless water supply; it seemed like the worst might already be behind them.

He took a long drink and wandered back to the bank, shaking the water from his back before lying down in the sunshine. As the sun warmed his skin, his eyes began to close, heightening the sound of Bongo still splashing in the shallows. He was just starting to drift off when Bongo emerged from the river, walked up alongside him and shook himself violently, sending a shower of water all over Horatio.

"Did you have to do that right *there*?" he asked, irritated to have been jolted from his tranquillity.

"I've got to dry off, haven't I?"

Bongo lay down a short way from Horatio, and for a while, the two devils soaked up the sun, listening to the sound of the river flowing by.

Bongo let his mind wander to thoughts of Tasmania. The rich forests, the mountains, the paths that led to his waterholes, and especially his family and friends. He missed them all, but he didn't want to tell Horatio that. Horatio would only laugh at him. He was a devil and that meant there was no place for sentimental thoughts, but he wondered how they were ever going to get home.

He had done a foolish thing at the Divide. That stupid prank with the bridge had almost cost him his only friend. Horatio had made that clear enough at the time, 'We're the only two devils here!' he had shouted. And if anything happened to Horatio, he would be alone in this wilderness. The only one of his kind.

Horatio had his faults, to be sure, being from the south, for one, but he was smart. Far smarter than Bongo considered himself to be, and if anyone could get them back to Tasmania, surely Horatio could.

He thought back to the long journey through the dusty land and wondered why he was chosen for the ooze. Why him? There were plenty of other devils they could have chosen, stronger, smarter devils. It didn't make any sense.

His grandfather used to say, 'Everything happens for a reason and the reason will reveal itself when it's good and ready'. He wondered if that was true. But as he looked out across the wide, flowing river, he couldn't help but think it would be quite some time before the reason was 'good and ready'.

When Horatio finally woke, Bongo was standing on the bank, first looking across the river, then upstream, then away from the river, then downstream. He watched Bongo make two or three revolutions and wondered how long he'd been doing that. Though he wasn't sure he wanted to hear the answer, he couldn't hold back his curiosity.

"What are you doing?"

"I'm trying to figure out which way we should go to get home. I feel like we're at a crossroads."

"I'd say we're at a river, but go on."

"Okay, so here's what we know. The sun rises in the east and sets in the west."

"Yes. And?"

"And we want to go to Tasmania."

"Bravo. And we're lost."

"Yes."

"And we don't know if Tasmania is north or south of where we are."

"No, we don't."

"And we don't know if Tasmania is east or west of where we are."

"No."

"So what do you think we should do?"

Bongo stood still and looked at Horatio. "Well, we don't want to go west because that's where we came from, and that's definitely not the right direction. That only leaves east, north or south. I say we take a 50:50 and go north."

"I'm not sure how choosing one direction out of three would be a 50:50," said Horatio wearily, "but what about north-east? Or south-east? Or north by north-east? Or..."

"Okay, okay," replied an irritated Bongo. "I'm trying to figure this out! Really, you and your big head, you think you're so smart!"

"You've got the big head. Your head is huge. Massive, actually. And there's nothing in it. All that wasted space. Why don't you do something useful with it and rent it out to some possums or something?"

"If you're not going to help, why don't you just butt out?"

"Bongo," Horatio said quietly, "we're lost. Really lost. There's no one here who even knows about Tasmania. There's no one we can ask, we've got no idea where we are and no idea which way to go to get home. We don't even know how far we need to travel to get back. For all we know, we could walk for the rest of our lives and still not find our way home. You've got to face the facts. The chances of us ever getting back to Tasmania are zero."

Bongo allowed the words to sink in as though they held some kind of truth just because Horatio had said them.

"What about our friends and family? What about them?"

"They're gone, Bongo. We're never going to see them again. Get that into your head. Sorry to be so blunt, but hoping you can somehow pick the right direction to get us home is just not going to happen. I don't like it any more than you do, but we are never going to see our friends, our families, or Tasmania again."

Bongo sat down and stared across the river as Horatio's words crumbled his hopes. He looked at the other bank and the distance to the other side. He thought of his family and the distance between them. He wondered what they must be thinking and whether they even cared that he was gone.

Of course they cared.

He cared. Why wouldn't they?

He had to find a way back to them, no matter how difficult the task. Suddenly, he knew exactly what he had to do. The hardest thing. He had to cross the river, if only to prove that he could do it. Without really knowing why, he knew that was the way to start the journey home.

"Do you have any kids?" he asked.

"Yeah, half a dozen or so. Why?"

"Well, so do I. And I'm not going to just give up on them. I'm going back, no matter how long it takes. And the first thing I'm going to do is cross this stupid river." Bongo got to his feet and started walking downstream, leaving Horatio in the grass.

"Where are you going?" Horatio shouted after him.

"Where does it look like I'm going? I'm going to look for a place to cross."

Horatio lay there for a moment wondering if he'd have to spend the rest of his life with that crazy animal. He knew it didn't matter which way they went, they would just be walking to somewhere else, when they should be searching for food. But he couldn't let Bongo just wander off.

"Bongo, wait!"

Bongo stopped and looked back. "What?" he shouted.

"If you want to cross the river, it would be better to go upstream. The river should be more narrow up there."

DARKNESS

Caper woke as the sun rose on the second day after the attack. He felt tired and weak, but at least he was alive, which was more than could be said for Shar. He looked over to see two shiny black crows picking at Shar's remains. No doubt they'd been busy while he slept.

"You got what you deserved, Shar," he thought, the ache in his side reminding him of the attack in the wallaby's den. He had been badly wounded, but the bleeding had finally stopped, leaving dark, matted patches of bloodied fur. As he lay there, his head still resting on the ground, he caught sight of the two echidna spines that had been lodged in his side.

Suddenly, the full weight of his humiliation returned. How could he have let a wallaby stand over him, pin him to the ground by the neck, and decide whether he would live or die? A wallaby! The thought sickened him.

He wondered how many times the wallaby had already told the story. He was probably bragging about it right now, telling everyone how he had conquered a dingo. Caper let out a growl of frustration and rage.

"That little weakling will wish he'd killed me," he said, swearing he would set the record straight the next time they met.

But while vengeance filled his thoughts, he was aware of what lay ahead of him. He had no idea how long he had been asleep, and he was still weak from the loss of blood. His wounds had begun to heal, but his injured side was still tender and he knew he was in no state to hunt. Worse still, he knew that every passing hour put more distance between him and the wallabies.

It wasn't going to be easy now.

Relentless. The word flashed in his mind, snapping him back to focus. He remembered his promise to Knuth. No matter how long it took, he would find that wallaby and settle the score.

But first he needed to heal himself, and for that he needed food. He dragged himself to his feet and looked over at what was left of Shar. It wasn't the most appealing meal, especially after the crows had torn into it, but it was a whole lot better than nothing.

He stumbled over to the carcass and began picking through the bones.

CRASH

It was Ned who started it. Out of boredom and out of the blue, he jumped over the top of Ellin, timing the peak of his jump just as her feet touched the ground. He laughed, bounded a short way, then jumped back over. Ellin giggled at the acrobatics, and soon the other wallabies were trying it.

The leaping quickly developed into a game. The wallabies would travel in single file, and the one in last place would zigzag up the side of the line, timing it just right to leap over each wallaby in turn, just as their feet touched the ground between hops. There were plenty of near misses and minor collisions to keep it exciting, and the distance began to fly by under their feet.

Even Wally played. Despite his troublesome knee, the game looked like too much fun to resist. He took his turn with the others, zigzagging up the line. But toward the end of the day, as tiredness set in and his concentration began to waver, his knee grew more erratic. It was late afternoon when it gave way in spectacular fashion.

He was nearing the front of the line, timing his

jumps perfectly, until he was two wallabies from the front. He coiled his legs for the next jump, but the moment he launched, he felt his knee collapse. Instead of jumping over Wiru, he drove straight into her, sending her crashing into the dirt. Jake didn't react fast enough to avoid the crash and ploughed into Wally, sending him tumbling into the ground. Ellin crashed into Jake, and by then, there were wallabies everywhere and no way to slow down to avoid them. Ned crashed into the pile and went flying off into the bush. Only Agnes, who had been preparing for her run up the side, managed to avoid the pile-up.

Peg, who was leading at the time, quickly realised that something had gone wrong from the noise of the crash. She stopped and bounced back to the tangled mess of wallabies still lying on the ground. "What on earth happened?" she asked.

"Do you really need to ask?" replied Wally, humiliated by the crash. He turned first to Wiru, who had taken the brunt of the collision. "Sorry, Wiru. Are you okay? I feel like such a klutz."

"I think so," she replied. "Maybe a little winded. I wasn't expecting that."

Wally was surprised she wasn't angry; he had just ploughed into her at almost full speed. He turned to the others.

"Sorry, everyone. That was my fault. Is everyone alright?"

"Oh yes, just a mild concussion," Jake replied,

hamming it up. "I'll be okay once I get my vision back."

Ellin quickly picked up on Jake's teasing. "No worries here except for some internal bleeding and a dislocated shoulder. Pop that back in for me, will you, Ned?"

"I'd love to," said Ned, "but I lost the use of both my arms in the crash. Can't feel a thing, actually. Totally numb. I'll probably be hospitalised for weeks."

The laughter grew with each exaggeration. Luckily, everyone was all right, because it had been an almighty tumble. There were a few bruises here and there, but none bigger than the bruise to Wally's confidence.

"It might be time to stop for the day," said Peg, realising everyone was tired. "We've covered a lot of ground. Let's head back to the river for a drink and call it a day."

A chorus of agreement rose from the group as they rose and dusted themselves off. Peg turned and led the way back towards the river. Wally let the others go past him as they joined in and followed Peg. Jake came through last and stopped beside Wally.

"You alright, mate?" he asked.

"Yeah, good enough," Wally said irritably. "Just ego damage really. I've hit the ground harder than that before, but I feel pretty stupid for breaking up the game. I probably shouldn't have been playing with this knee of mine."

"Don't be too hard on yourself. Someone was bound to cause a crash sooner or later. That's what made it fun." Jake smiled. "Come on, let's go find that river."

The Hardest Thing

A short way upstream, Horatio found what he was looking for. The river cut through the land in two sweeping bends, connected by a long, straight stretch of water. At the outside edge of each of the bends, the river slowed and became shallow, due to the silt that was deposited by the slowing of the river.

"Okay, here's what we do," said Horatio. "See that bend in the river up ahead?"

"Yes."

"We walk out as far as we can in the shallows on this side, then swim like mad across the current. If we keep swimming, the river should pick us up and swing us out into the shallows of the bend on the other side. Does that make sense?"

"Yes. There's only one problem."

"Only one? That's a relief," said Horatio. "What is it?"

"I can't really swim," replied Bongo.

"What? Of course you can. All Tasmanian devils can swim."

"I mean, I can swim, but I've never swum anything that wide, flowing that fast before."

"How did you think we were going to get across?"

"I was kind of hoping for a bridge or something."

"A bridge? Where are you going to find a bridge?"

"We found one at that ramp."

"Which you quickly destroyed."

"Well, maybe we should go further upstream, maybe we haven't looked hard enough, walked far enough, you know..."

"Bongo, you won't find another magical bridge. If you want to cross the river, you're going to have to do it the hard way and swim. I think we can make it. But here's a tip: if you don't make it across to the other side, you'll be swept down the river, and who knows where you'll end up or whether you'll be alive when you get there. So don't muck around. When you get in the water, swim like a devil possessed."

Bongo looked out across the river in silence, contemplating what he was about to do.

"Look, you'll be fine," Horatio said. "Just kick

your legs as hard and as fast as you can. We'll be across in no time. Come on, let's get up to that first bend."

Horatio trotted off, leaving Bongo behind.

Bongo took one last, long look at the river. "This is how I get home," he thought, charging himself with courage. He turned and ran to catch up to Horatio.

When they reached the first bend, Horatio waded out into the shallows. The water was flowing fast, but they made good headway by the time they were in up to their chests.

"Are you sure you want to do this?" he shouted over the rushing water.

Bongo didn't take his eyes off the river. "Yes."

He braced himself against the water's flow, knowing that as soon as he relaxed, it would sweep him away. "I'll go first."

"Just kick your legs as hard as you can. You'll be fine."

Bongo paused, as the fear started to seep into the cracks in his confidence. But if Horatio thought this was the best place to cross, then this was probably his best chance. His fear was weighing him down. He had to act. Right now.

"Geronimo!" he yelled, throwing himself headlong into the water. The river had him immediately, tumbling him and pushing him under. He quickly righted himself and lifted his head out of the water, spluttering for air. The struggle was on.

Horatio saw the river was pulling Bongo too quickly downstream. He wasn't kicking his back legs.

"Your back legs! Kick your back legs!" he shouted.

Bongo flailed about in the water, oblivious to the instructions. Horatio hurled himself into the river and swam hard with the current down to Bongo. He pushed his shoulder into Bongo's rump.

"Your back legs, Bongo! Kick your back legs!"

Bongo's panic shattered at the sound of Horatio's voice. His back legs flew into action.

"Yes! Yes! Harder!" yelled Horatio, swimming across the current with all his strength.

The devils fought against the force of the river, their progress spurring them on. They began to feel the current ease as they were swung into the far bend.

"Don't stop until you can feel the bottom!" Horatio shouted. The last thing he wanted to see was Bongo being dragged back out and washed downstream.

Horatio felt his toes scrape the bottom, and with one final push he was standing in the shallows.

"Come on, Bongo, you're nearly there!"

Bongo was exhausted. His muscles ached, his limbs begged for rest, but he knew he couldn't stop. The current carried him past Horatio and further downstream. He could feel himself slipping back into the flow as Horatio's warning echoed in his head: 'If you don't make it across to the other side, you'll be swept down the river and who knows where you'll end up or whether you'll be alive when you get there.'

He swam with everything he had left, his limbs thrashing until finally he overcame the river's flow. He didn't stop until his ankles were above the waterline. He collapsed in the shallows, gasping for air, totally spent.

"We made it. We're on our way," he thought, as the water lapped at his ears.

Horatio ran over to make sure Bongo was all right.

"Don't they teach you to swim in the North?" he asked.

"We don't have rivers like that."

"And just so I know, why exactly did we have to cross the river?"

"I had to do something," Bongo replied breathlessly. "The hardest thing. I couldn't help thinking the river stood in our way. Maybe not in the way of us getting home, just in the way. And we crossed it. What could possibly stand in our way now?"

Horatio stared at Bongo lying there in the water, trying to decide whether that was the stupidest or most logical thing he'd ever heard. He turned and climbed up onto the bank, shaking himself to dry off.

"Well, come on, then. Let's go find something to eat."

SPOILS OF VENGEANCE

"Hey, quiet for a second," said Horatio suddenly, interrupting Bongo's latest monologue. "I think I hear something."

The two devils had been walking away from the river when Horatio heard the voices coming from behind a small mound. He crept up the side and peered over the edge. On the other side were four wild dogs, bragging about a feast they'd just had at a place called Rocky Hill.

"That was too easy," said one. "It was like they were just sitting there waiting for us to arrive. When they saw how many of us there were, they just gave up. One of them, an ugly thing with beady little eyes, just stood there all hunched over. Didn't even move when I went for him. I finished him off real quick."

"I know," said another. "But there were too many of us this time. We absolutely decimated the mob. Some of those dogs just flew into a frenzy, killing everything in sight. I don't even know how many of those wallabies are left. Not many, I'd say. I saw a bunch take off into the hills, but it's not going to be so easy to catch them now that they're all spread out. We should've done what we usually do and just picked off enough to eat."

"Nah, that was too much fun. Going crazy with a huge pack like that? How often do you get a chance to do that?"

"Once, I'd say. It's all over now."

"They'll come back."

"I doubt it. We're going to have to follow them into the hills and do all the legwork just to find them. That won't be anywhere near as easy. And look at the size of our pack now, it's huge. How long do you think the rest of those wallabies will last with all those dogs after them?"

"What's going on?" Bongo whispered as he crawled up alongside Horatio.

"It's a pack of wild dogs. They're talking about some place called Rocky Hill. We'd better get out of here. We don't want to mess with that lot."

"Why?" asked Bongo. "I could take them."

"You could not 'take them'."

"Oh yeah? Well, why don't we find out. How about I chuck a rock at that big one and see what happens?"

"How about you don't! Who do you think you are?"

"Bongo the Brave. I just crossed that river. I can do anything."

"You'd be halfway down that river, drowned, if it wasn't for me. Now just be quiet, will you? Let's head back to the river and follow it until we're clear of these guys. There might be more of them in the area."

Horatio turned and scampered down the mound as Bongo took one last look at the pack. Horatio was right, they didn't look too friendly. Bongo reminded himself that he didn't need any more trouble. His job was to get home. He quickly turned and followed Horatio back to the river.

Horatio found a trail that followed the river bank, eventually leading to a stretch littered with wallaby footprints.

"Hey, have you noticed all the footprints?" asked Bongo.

"Yes."

"Well, they're going the other way."

"Yes."

"Well, if we are looking for food, shouldn't we be going the other way too?"

Horatio stopped and turned. "Look, we just overheard a few wild dogs talking about a huge pack of wild dogs and a wallaby feast. The wallabies going back that way were probably part of that feast. I don't want to get mixed up with those dogs, so we need to put some distance between us and them. That's why we're going this way. Okay?"

"But maybe there would be some leftovers. I'm starving."

"Bongo, I'm hungry too, but it's not worth it. We'll find something a little further on."

"You'd better be right. Remember, you're a Tasmanian devil. You're not supposed to be afraid of anything."

"I'm a Tasmanian devil, all right," replied Horatio, "but you'd better get it into your thick skull, we're not in Tasmania anymore."

* * *

Caper had been resting in the afternoon sun when the creature wandered into the clearing. He hadn't heard the animal approach over the sound of the waterfall, but suddenly his senses were on full alert. Had his luck finally changed? A fresh meal wandering into the open like that was an opportunity too good to miss. He rose quietly to his feet, ignoring the pain in his side. The animal hadn't noticed him; it seemed to only be interested in Shar's carcass.

Caper had the element of surprise.

He crept forward, preparing to attack.

"Bongo!" Horatio called when he saw the remains of Shar. "I think I've found something for lunch."

"So have I," thought Caper as he waited for his moment.

As Horatio pushed his nose into Shar's carcass, Caper lunged. Though he was still sore from his wounds, his attack was sharp. His jaws locked on the back of Horatio's thick neck, his teeth tearing into the skin. Horatio let out a ferocious growl, twisting to free himself, but Caper refused to let go.

Then, just as suddenly, another set of jaws clamped down on the back of Caper's neck. He yelped in pain as Bongo's sharp teeth sank into the skin behind his ears, releasing his grip on Horatio.

Horatio found his feet and threw himself back into the melee.

Bongo flipped Caper onto his back and Horatio went straight for the underside of Caper's neck. His jaws snapped shut in a death grip, strangling the small dingo. Caper struggled violently, but it was only a matter of time before his breath finally ran out.

"Stone the crows," said Horatio, nursing the gash on his neck. "I didn't see that coming."

"Are you all right?" asked Bongo. "Your neck is bleeding."

"I'll be fine," replied Horatio, playing down the wound. "It's just a nick here and there."

Bongo looked down at Caper's lifeless body.

"That must be one of those dingers that kangaroo was talking about."

"For a start," Horatio began patiently, "it's a ding*o*, not a ding*er*, and it wasn't a kangaroo that we met, it was a wallaby."

"Looked like a kangaroo to me."

"I'm sure it did. But I can assure you, it was a wallaby."

"What makes you so sure about that?"

"Wallabies have a different body shape. They're smaller, have shorter legs and a shorter nose. And besides that, he told us he was a wallaby."

"You're making that up," said Bongo, still unsure if he could tell the difference between a wallaby and a kangaroo. "Anyway, that's the end of that dinger or whatever it was. You were lucky he didn't do more damage."

"Yes, I am," said Horatio. "And thank you for coming to help. I mean that. It was nice to have a moment when we weren't fighting each other for a change."

"No worries. It looked like you needed help."

"Well, I'm not sure I needed help. But thank you for helping anyway. He certainly took me by surprise."

"He had you pinned."

"He had me momentarily pinned, but I'm sure

I could have freed myself."

"*Sure* you could have. If it wasn't for me, you'd be dead."

"Oh, alright! Thank you for saving me, Bongo the Brave, you big hero. Now how about you fill that big mouth of yours with some lunch? There's plenty here."

The devils made a feast of Caper, gorging on the fresh meat until they'd had their fill.

"Oh, my stomach," groaned Bongo.

"Mine too. I couldn't eat another thing."

"But there's still some left."

"Don't. I'll be sick if I eat any more."

Bongo wandered through the clearing to find a spot to lie down when he noticed the bloodied echidna quills that Wally had extracted from Caper's side.

"Hey look," said Bongo, picking up the spines and handing one to Horatio. "Toothpicks!"

The sun began to set on the devils as they lay in the clearing, letting at least some of the meal go down, when Horatio finally spoke.

"We'd better move away from the food. There will be other animals coming around soon, and we don't know what kind or how many. Besides, it's starting to look like rain."

"Oh, I was almost asleep. Do we really have to

go? Shouldn't we guard the food?"

"If we were in Tasmania, I'd say yes. But we're not. It's better to be safe than sorry, especially with those wild dogs prowling around. Let's just go and find somewhere to sleep. We can come back in the morning if we're still hungry. But I can't even think about food right now, I'm stuffed."

Bongo struggled to his feet with a contented smile wide across his face. "Okay. Which way?"

"Let's go this way," Horatio said, pointing downstream. "The noise of that waterfall is going to drive me crazy."

They wandered along the same track Caper and Shar had followed on the way to Gus's. The trail led along a ridge that dropped away steeply on one side, all the way to the bottom of the waterfall.

"Hey Horatio, now that I've saved your life and we're best friends and all, can I ask you something?"

"Ah, you're pushing your luck with the 'saved my life' thing and even more with the idea that we're best friends. And I know I'm going to regret this, but yes, fire away. Ask me anything."

"So," began Bongo, hesitating, "it's about your name."

"What about my name?"

"It's 'Horatio'."

"What's wrong with that?"

"It sounds a bit la-di-da for a Tasmanian devil, don't you think? Too, I don't know, fancy pants."

"Pompous? Is that the word you are looking for? You're not the first to suggest my name may not be the most appropriate for a Tasmanian devil, but my mother gave me that name. It's my name, and that's all there is to say about it."

"Can I shorten it a little? Make it more Australian?"

"What are you suggesting?" Horatio braced himself for what was coming.

"How about 'Hozza'?"

"Oh lord," said Horatio, looking down at his feet, "take me now."

"Is that a 'yes'?"

Horatio looked up and saw a hollow log just big enough for a Tasmanian devil or two.

"No, that is not a 'yes'. There's a hollow log over there. That will do for tonight."

BLUE BELLY JOE

Travelling now was nothing like travelling through the west. The bush had thickened further, especially around the river, and the dense scrub had slowed their pace considerably. Whenever they found high ground, the wallabies tried to map out a path that would let them move quickly while still following the river, but it had become increasingly difficult. Often, they had no choice but to make the best of it and push their way through the scrub.

The effort began to wear some of the wallabies down, the slow progress, the branches scratching their skin, the rough ground underfoot. Although Wally knew the dense bush wouldn't last forever, he could sense the spirit in the group starting to falter. Fortunately, after days of battling the thick undergrowth, he came across a trail that cut through the scrub.

"Over here!" he called, looking back. "I think I've found a trail."

"Really? Are you sure you want to go down there?"

The voice startled Wally. He swung around to see a large woolly animal sitting beside the track. He was so well hidden in the bush that Wally hadn't even noticed him.

"Where did *you* come from?" Wally asked.

"Where did *I* come from? I've been here the whole time. Never mind where I came from, where do you think *you're* going?"

"We're going to the ocean."

"The ocean? What's the ocean?"

"I don't know," Wally replied. "It's a long story."

"Bit dangerous, isn't it? Going somewhere you don't know?"

"Not really. Well, sometimes."

"Well, which is it?"

"We've been travelling for a while now. We're getting used to it."

"Seems like a crazy idea to me. What if you don't get there?"

"We'll get there."

"How do you know? What if you get lost?"

"We just have to follow the river."

"What if the river dries up?"

"Have you seen how much water is in that river? It's not going to dry up."

"What if there's a flash drought?"

"A what?"

"Or worse, a flash flood and the river changes direction? What will you do then?"

Wally just stared blankly at the animal, unsure how to respond.

"Or what if the sun doesn't rise tomorrow and you can't see? Or you trip over and break your leg, or worse, hit your head on a rock and both your eyeballs fall out? You won't be able to see then, will you? How will you know which way to go? Oh, I'd say it's a bit dangerous all right. The whole idea sounds stone cold crazy. Just like your ears."

"There's nothing wrong with my ears."

"Yes there is. You've got crazy ears. One's bigger than the other. Probably affects your thinking. What are you going to do if you travel all that way across the countryside and you finally get there and it's not what you expected? What then?"

Wally looked at the animal patiently. "How will I know it's not what I expect if I don't get there in the first place? Anyway, none of that matters. That's where we're going."

"Who's we?"

Just then, Agnes came around the bend and joined Wally, staring at the strange animal.

"Oh, I see you brought your sister."

Then Ned and Wiru arrived.

"…and your brother and cousin, no doubt…"

Then Peg.

"…and your niece, I presume…"

Then Jake and Ellin.

"…and I suppose these are your grandparents. You have a big family. How many more are there? By the way, you two look a little young to be grandparents."

"Who is this bloke?" Jake asked.

"I'm Blue Belly Joe," announced the animal. "I'm a ram. A ram's ram. And if you don't show some respect, Grandpa, I'll show you the pointy end of my horns."

"What are you doing all the way out here, alone?" Wally asked.

"I escaped. I'm a free ram. Went over the wall by squeezing under the fence, I did. I'm on the run. I'm not much of a runner, but they'll never catch me alive. I'll spring into a billabong if I have to, I will. They'll hear my ghost as they pass by that billabong, I'll give you the drum. They'll be hearing that all day long. All. Day. Long."

There was a pause while the wallabies tried to fathom what the ram was talking about. Finally, Wally asked, "On the run from whom?"

"The farmer. Who do you think?"

"The farmer? What's a farmer?"

"He's the bloke that keeps the sheep. I'm a sheep. Rams are the blokes. The farmer locks the sheep in the paddock and cuts the wool off. Shears it right off your back, he does. Right off your back."

The ram leaned closer to Wally.

"I'm never going back. You have no idea what it's like to have all your wool cut off, especially in the middle of winter. It's humiliating and freezing."

"Why does he cut all your wool off?"

"No idea, mate. But I'm never getting shorn again. You watch out for that farmer. He's dangerous. Don't cross any fences. Don't eat in the paddocks."

"Okay, we'll keep our eyes out. Now if you don't mind, we'd best get on our way before we lose the afternoon."

"What? Down there?" said Blue Belly Joe, pointing down the track. "There's nothing down there but swamp. You don't want to go down there, unless you want to get to Kanandah."

"Kanandah?"

"Yes, yes. The island."

"An island? In the middle of a swamp?"

"No, no, no. You go through the swamp to get to the island. It's the only way to get there. The island is huge and it's smack bang in the middle of the river. I thought all you wallabies knew about it. They say it's a paradise. Lots of wallabies and no dingoes. They've got koalas and possums too, so your little mate there would be happy," he said, nodding towards Darcy.

"Well, thanks," said Wally, "but we aren't going to an island. We're following the river to the ocean."

"Then you've got a long walk ahead of you. You can either walk around the swamp, through the thickest bush I've ever seen, or go back the way you came, about two days back, then take the track north over the ridge and go the long way around."

Suddenly Peg piped up. "About this island," she began. "Are the wallabies friendly?"

"They seem to be, at least the ones that come through here are."

Wally looked at Peg and knew what was coming.

"And is it green?" she continued.

"Well, they keep going back."

"And there are no dingoes, you say."

"That's what they tell me. I've never been there. I can't get through the swamp with these confounded hooves, I just sink."

"And there's only one way to get there, through the swamp?"

"Apparently. At least, one way for wallabies. I'm not sure how the koalas and possums got over there, probably some tree, somewhere. Blasted possums find a way to go everywhere."

Peg turned to Wally. "Wally, this sounds like it's exactly what we've been looking for. A place free of dingoes, with food and water, and protected by a swamp. It sounds perfect!"

"I agree with Peg," said Ned. "It does sound pretty good."

The agreement rippled through the rest of the mob.

"And I can tell you now, no one wants to go the long way around."

Wally looked at Ned, then back at the rest of the mob.

"Look," he said under his breath, "this bloke obviously has a few screws loose. Think about it. He's going to walk us into a swamp to find some magical island paradise in the middle of a river. It sounds a bit far-fetched, don't you think?"

"But what if he's telling the truth? What if the island is real?" asked Peg.

"What if it's not and we get stranded in the middle of a swamp?" Wally looked at her, seeing her hope overcome her reason. He turned back to the ram.

"So if we wanted to go to this island, how would we get there?"

"Keep going down this path," said the ram. "You're heading straight into a swamp. As you walk along the edge of the swamp, you'll come to two stones. Big stones. They look like..., like..." He struggled to find the word. "Rocks. The two stones look like rocks. Big rocks. You can't miss them.

"Now this is the important part. There's a way through the swamp, but it's treacherous, it's the only path in the swamp that will hold your weight. If you stray off the path, there's plenty of mud and quicksand to swallow you up. And if you miss a turn, you'll never find your way back out. You mark my words, there are plenty of animals lying at the bottom of that swamp."

"And how do we find this path?"

"You can't see it, it's under the water, and the water is thick and murky. You've just got to feel your way, and follow these directions.

"Enter the swamp between the stones. You'll feel the path under your feet. Then go straight until the first big fork in the path. Take the right fork, then another right fork, then left. Then left, right, left. You'll see a big old log lying in the swamp. A family of mudskippers used to live there but they left months ago, right after the last downpour. Just up and left, and headed out towards the river, or so I'm told. But you probably don't care about that, right?

"So right after the log it's left, left and then two rights. That will lead you to the causeway between the swamp and the island. Be careful getting across there, the water flows pretty quickly, and the rocks are covered in moss. Very slippery. Once you cross the causeway you're home and hosed. Have you got all that?"

Wally looked at the ram with a glazed look on his face. He turned to the group. "Did you guys get all that?"

The response from the mob was affirmative, but uncertain.

"So how do you know all this?" Wally asked. "If you've never actually been there."

"I keep my ear to the ground, sunshine, my ear to the ground. I've seen wallabies heading to the island. They all come this way because the passage through the swamp is the only way to get there. I wanted to go myself, so I asked a few for directions, but like I said, my hooves just sink into the mud."

"It sounds perfect, Wally," Peg enthused. "Let's go and take a look."

"I don't know, Peg. It sounds pretty risky to me. Wandering into a swamp to get to a place based on a story from some guy who hasn't even been there. What if it's just a story?"

"But what if it's not? What if it's all true? We gambled on the Divide, didn't we? Wasn't that just a story too?"

"Yes, but there were kangaroos going there.

This is different."

"Not to me." Peg turned to the others. "Who thinks we should try to find this island?"

A short discussion broke out between the wallabies as they weighed the risks of the swamp against the prospect of having to backtrack and spend days going the long way around. Ultimately, it was a simple decision. All the Rocky Hill wallabies wanted to go. Peg wanted to go. Jake didn't really care but he didn't want to go the long way around.

Apart from Wally, it was unanimous. Wally's resistance appeared to mean nothing to the group.

"All right then," he said. "It looks like we're going."

Ned turned to the ram. "Down this way, you said?"

"That's right. Look for the two big stones."

Ned walked past the ram and started down the path, the rest of the mob following closely behind.

"Oh, one more thing," the ram called out after them. "Beware of the snakes. That swamp is full of them."

THE WOODEN EAGLE

The great tree had grown out of the incline, struggling to find the sun while anchoring itself in what little soil it could find on the side of the slope. Having tethered itself to the hillside, the base of the trunk had curved sharply away from the roots, which now reached out like hands full of withering fingers. The tree had fallen long ago, deflected by other trees competing for the sunlight as it fell. It now lay still and broken across the forest floor. Over time, the tree had begun to return itself to the undergrowth. The centre of the trunk was now hollow and had been for years, providing refuge to any animals in need of shelter.

Horatio walked carefully down the slope and cautiously made his way into the log, making sure no other animals had already claimed the shelter as their own.

"Hurry up and get in there!" said Bongo impatiently. "I'm tired!"

"Just wait a minute, for heaven's sake. You

don't want to find yourself sleeping with a snake, do you?"

"Oh, a snake. What are you scared of a little snake for?" Bongo said, giving Horatio a shove.

"Hey!"

Horatio moved further into the log, though it was almost impossible to see. His body blocked what little daylight managed to filter through the clouds in the fading twilight.

"It looks empty," he said, lying down.

Bongo followed him in. "Move further in, will you? My back feet are barely inside."

"Well, maybe you shouldn't have eaten so much," Horatio muttered, as he slid further into the log.

"Come on, it's starting to rain."

The first drops of a new shower began to fall as the pair curled up in the log.

"Perfect timing," said Horatio with a yawn, as the rain began drumming a natural lullaby on the trunk.

Bongo rolled onto his back, his full belly pointing skyward. He couldn't help thinking things were finally starting to work out. It seemed crossing the river had somehow set them on their way home. No matter how pointless Horatio thought it was, to Bongo it was now just a matter of perseverance. He began to think once more of his home and family. "I'll see you again soon," he thought, as visions of his life in Tasmania filled his mind. His eyes began to close, and soon both devils were fast asleep, bellies full and lost in their dreams, as the rain began to fall more heavily outside.

*   *   *

It was a peaceful sleep, curled up in the warmth of the log, and the night passed quickly. But as the morning broke and the last drops of rain fell, Horatio began his morning stretch, accidentally kicking Bongo in the face.

"Hey!" Bongo shouted, shoving the foot back. "Watch where you're putting your big feet!"

"Stop pushing!" Horatio snapped, his moment of peace already lost. He kicked the foot back in retaliation, and suddenly all the mateship from the day before evaporated into yet another devil brawl.

Bongo lunged at Horatio, who shoved him against the downhill side of the log, and that was all it took to set the log in motion.

The whole trunk began to roll slowly, the floor of the hollow remaining on the slope as the rotted wood came away from the rest of the log. The devils rolled with it, suddenly lying on what had been their roof only moments before, staring up at the clouds that still rolled across the sky. The curved base of the trunk now pointed upward, like the bow of a grand ship, as the slick, rain-soaked undergrowth gave way beneath it.

The log inched forward slowly at first, scraping against an old tree that pushed the back of the log outwards, directing the bow straight down the hill.

"Oh no," Horatio groaned, the dread of what was about to happen rippling through him. He reached for something to hold onto, but his paws just filled with the rotten wood left over from where the rest of the trunk used to be.

"Hold on!" he shouted, as the point of no return was lost to history.

The log gathered speed down the slope like a runaway canoe, flattening small trees and bouncing violently against larger trees, sending wood chips flying. The devils wailed in fear as the log thundered through the trees, gaining momentum down the steep, slippery slope.

Horatio stared wide-eyed as the forest flashed past him, waiting for the fatal collision that could only be moments away.

"Bongo! We're going to have to jump!"

"Jump? Are you crazy? We're going too fast!"

"There's no other waaaaaaaaayyyyy..."

The curve of the bow crashed into something solid lying across their path, launching the runaway sled into the sky. The impact sent both devils crashing into the front of the log, giving them a perfect view backwards of the land disappearing behind them. The log flew through the air, tail down, like a giant wooden eagle coming in to land.

"Nooooooooooo!" Horatio screamed as the log began its descent. The horrifying moments passed in slow motion. Both devils braced for impact.

The tail of the log hit the water first, skidding across the surface. The bow descended, touching down in an almost perfect landing. Water sprayed everywhere, soaking the devils to the skin. Finally, the makeshift canoe came to rest in the lake, just beyond the waterfall, the bow standing proudly out of the water, the stern partially submerged.

The two devils stared wide-eyed at each other, then Bongo burst into a fit of uncontrollable laughter.

"What on earth is so funny?"

"That was awesome!" Bongo cried.

Horatio stared down in disbelief, watching Bongo roll around in the bottom of the log. But as he watched, he couldn't help but break into a smile himself. "Yes. That was quite exhilarating, wasn't it?" he said, the fear forgotten, his smile turning to a chuckle, the chuckle to full-blown laughter. Soon both devils were laughing hysterically on the bottom of the floating log.

"You should have seen your face!" Bongo said,

tears streaming down his cheeks. "I thought your eyes were going to pop out of your head!"

There was nothing else to do but laugh. The sheer terror of the ride was over, and somehow, they had both survived.

Eventually, as the laughter began to subside, Horatio asked, "Okay, Bongo. What now? What's our next move?" as he broke into another fit of laughter.

"I don't know," said Bongo, looking over the side of the log as it floated in the lake, the tears of laughter still rolling down his face, "but I think it will have something to do with those rapids we are heading toward."

SWAMP

The wallabies found the entrance to the swamp easily; the two large stones stood out like a doorway to danger. Their legs were now caked in mud, the path having turned into a muddy bog well before they'd reached the stone markers. Between the stones was an open marsh, full of long, tall reeds that stretched well above the wallabies' heads, divided by a narrow, watery path that split the marsh in two. The reeds swayed in the afternoon breeze, the gentle rustling inviting the wallabies into the swamp like a siren's call, disguising the danger that lay within.

"Are you sure this is the place?" Wiru asked, peering into the swamp.

"It must be," replied Peg. "It's the only place we've seen with two obvious stones, and we're running out of trail. We must be almost surrounded by swamp now."

They looked into the swamp with growing unease. It had sounded so easy when the ram explained the directions. They now faced an altogether different reality.

"Are you sure you want to do this?" Wally asked.

"Yes," Peg answered quickly.

"Okay then, who's going first?"

"I'll go," said Ned, stepping forward. He went between the stones and into the swamp.

"I can feel the path," he called back, his body sinking up to his haunches in the muddy water. "It feels solid under my feet."

He inched forward, the water now up to his elbows, while the others watched, half expecting him to disappear into the muddy water at any moment.

"Okay," Peg said nervously, "I'm going in." She followed Ned's path into the swamp. Darcy left her pouch and scrambled up to her shoulders.

The rest of the wallabies looked at one another.

"Here goes nothing," said Wiru, heading in next, followed by the rest of the Rocky Hill wallabies, then Jake, and finally Wally.

"I sure hope there aren't any crocodiles in here," Wally quipped as he stepped into the water.

"Don't even joke about it," Jake said, the eeriness of the swamp already setting him on edge.

Ellin, just ahead of Jake, turned and shot Wally a filthy look.

Their progress was slow, but the wallabies had no trouble following the directions. The first fork in the path was obvious, and Ned took the right fork. Then another right, then a left. Then a left, a right, and another left. Finally, an old log, lying in the swamp, came into view, right next to another fork in the reeds, just as the ram had said.

"The log!" Peg cried. "Ned, you've found it! Now just two lefts and two rights to go."

"Wait a minute," said Ned. "Wasn't there a right before the two lefts?"

"No," said Peg. "The ram said, 'Right after the log it's two lefts'."

"No, I thought he said, 'Right after the log, *then* two lefts'. I think we go right."

"Are you sure? I don't think that's what he said."

Wiru, following close behind, chimed in. "I thought he said, 'Right after the log, it's two lefts', too."

She turned to Agnes. "Do you think the ram said 'Right after the log it's two lefts' or 'Right after the log then two lefts'?"

"What's the difference?" asked Agnes.

"Ellin?"

"I don't know, all I heard was the first right,

right, left, blah, blah, blah..."

Jake piped up. "He definitely said, 'Right after the log'."

"Yes, but what did he say after that?"

"Then it was two lefts, I'm pretty sure, so it should be right, right?"

"Oh great," said Agnes. "That means two of us think we need to go right and two of us think we should go left. What do you think the ram said, Wally?"

"I've got no idea. I wanted to go around the swamp, so I wasn't really listening. But while we've been trying to decide which way to go, a big snake has just slithered up that branch sticking out of the log."

They all turned to see a large swamp python coiling itself lazily along the branch.

"Helloooooo," he said, drawing out the greeting in a deep, velvety voice. "Have you all lost your waaaaay?" A smile creased his cheeks and a long, forked tongue flashed between his lips.

"We're not lost, just deciding," replied Ned.

"Perhaps I can help," offered the snake. "I know this swamp very well. Very well indeeeeeed."

"Thanks, but we don't need your help. We're doing fine by ourselves. Besides, we were told to be wary of the snakes in the swamp."

"And who told you that?" the snake asked defensively. "Someone who hasn't met all the snakes in the swamp, I'm sure. We're not all bad, you know, but we all get tarred with the same horrid brush."

"Well, it's unsettling, the way you slither everywhere. All that slithering puts everyone off."

"What else are we supposed to do? We're just snakes. Born without arms and legs, trying to get by in this world the only way we can. Perhaps those who are put off by our slithering should try slithering for themselves. It's not easy, you know, but I understand. It makes us different, and a difference seems to be all the justification you need for persecution. Honestly. I'm so awfully tired of the stereotyping. In every single story we are the villains. Every single one! All the way back to Adam. We are always the ones you can't trust. It's ridiculous! And this business that we're frightening because we're slimy and we sneak up on things, well, we're not slimy at all. Touch me, if you don't believe me. And we sneak up on things because we have to eat. I make no apologies for that."

"Who's Adam?" Wiru asked.

"Adam. You know, Adam and Eeeeeve?"

"No."

"Well, never mind. The snake got the blame for that one too. It was just one apple, for heaven's sake..." The snake stared off into the distance as though justice would arrive from afar.

"Anyway," he said suddenly, "I presume you're all going to the island. I've seen wallabies pass through here before. You'll like it over there," he continued, his long tongue flashing between his lips again. "You need to go left."

Ned turned to Peg. "That proves it. The ram told us not to trust the snakes in the swamp. We should go right."

"That's right," Jake agreed.

By then, Wally had made his way to the front of the group and had approached the snake. He stopped about a metre from the snake's head, which now extended out from the branch as though it was suspended in the air. Wally looked straight into the reptile's eyes as they focused back on him, each animal trying to read the other. It was as close as he had ever been to a snake, especially one this large, and he knew the snake could have him wrapped in its coils in an instant, squeezing the life right out of him. He should have been afraid, but strangely, he felt no fear.

"Do you know what happened to the mudskippers that used to live in this log?" Wally asked.

"I ate them," the snake replied without hesitation. "They were delicious. The whole family."

Wally watched the snake's tongue flicker, tasting the air, their eyes still locked on each other. Finally, Wally turned to Ned and Peg.

"I'm going left."

"Wally! You heard what the ram said: 'Beware of the snakes'. Look at him! He makes my skin crawl. We can't trust anything he says."

"Then who should we trust? None of us can remember the directions exactly, and let's face it, he was a crackpot anyway. I'm going to trust myself. I'm going with the snake. You don't have to follow."

The wallabies watched as Wally took the left fork and quickly disappeared into the reeds. They waited as the sound of the swamp grew louder and louder, listening for Wally's cry for help as he was consumed by quicksand, or worse, but the only sound they heard was the hum of mosquitoes and the constant whirr of dragonflies.

"Seems very quiet, doesn't it?" asked the snake.

The waiting was too much for Jake. "I'm going after him," he said suddenly. "We should've heard something by now."

"Jake!" Peg called, "Just wait!"

"For what?" he said, pushing past the others, following Wally's path.

"Oh, not again!" Peg said in frustration. "One of these days, Wally..." She let the sentence trail off as she took the left fork. The Rocky Hill girls followed immediately after.

Ned took one last look at the snake. "You'd better not be lying."

The snake only smiled, his tongue still flickering between his scaly lips.

RAPIDS

"What?" asked Horatio as he looked over the side of the log. Just as suddenly as the laughter had started, it stopped, as Horatio tried to figure out how they were going to get through the rough water. His first thought was to abandon the log and swim, but he doubted there would be enough time to get to shore. The log was heading sideways into the rapids and he'd seen enough debris floating down the rivers in Tasmania to know that was not good. He had to find a way to steer the little raft. He clawed at the side of the log and managed to bend a small flat strip away from the rest of the wood.

"Bongo, help me break a piece off the side of the log."

There was urgency in Horatio's voice so Bongo jumped in to help without asking any questions. The devils hauled against the splintering wood until it snapped, sending both of them tumbling to the other side of the log.

"What did we do that for?" asked Bongo.

"To steer." Horatio picked up the piece of wood and pushed it into the water on one side. Immediately the log began to swing around and soon Horatio had the curve of the trunk pointing directly into the rapids.

"Hold on," he said. "Here we go."

The log rocked wildly as it bounced its way over and through the churning white-water. Bongo held onto whatever he could find as Horatio shuffled from side to side with the makeshift paddle, guiding the log through the least of the troubled waters.

When they finally emerged on the other side of the rapids, Horatio dug the paddle in and the log swung towards the shore.

"What are you doing?" Bongo asked.

"I'm beaching this thing. We have to get off."

"Why? We'd just have to walk then. Let's just ride it down the river, that's much easier."

"How do you know that's the right way to go?"

"It is. All we have to do is sail down the river. Don't ask me how I know, I just know."

Horatio sighed, dug the paddle in to right the trunk and moved it back into the flow in the middle of the river.

"If we're going to be sailing, I suppose we'll need a name for this fine vessel. Any ideas?"

Bongo asked.

"After what we just went through, how about The Wooden Eagle?"

"Perfect!"

Bongo moved up to the front of the log and looked over the bow. "Hoist the mainsail and scuttle the jib, Captain, we sail for Tasmania!" he cried, punching his paw into the air.

"What?" asked Horatio. "Do you even know what that means?"

"Nope," replied Bongo, "but that doesn't make me stupid because you don't know either."

Horatio just shook his head and with the paddle in hand, let the river carry them downstream.

KANANDAH

Wally made his way quietly through the swamp, taking the next fork left, then turning right and right again. He emerged onto a patch of mud, and there, a short way upstream, he saw the causeway, just as Jake caught up to him.

"Looks like you were right about the snake."

"Yeah. He wasn't so bad after all."

"How did you know he was telling the truth?"

"We'd barely said hello, and all he could talk about was how unfair it was that everyone hated snakes so much. Obviously, that was important to him. So, let's say he really does want to improve his reputation. If he tells us the right way to go and we follow it, he's done a good thing, and maybe we'll tell others about the friendly snake we met in the swamp.

"But if he tells us the right way and we second-guess him by going the other way, we'd die. From his perspective, that's our own fault. He might get a meal out of it, but his reputation doesn't change. And there's really nothing in it for him if he tells us to go the wrong way, especially if we second-guess him on that. Giving us the right direction is the only way he gets what he wants. Besides, I think he did eat those mudskippers. He didn't look hungry; I don't think he has any trouble finding food."

"I never would have thought of all that."

Just then, Peg came through the reeds, and she was not happy.

"Wally, one of these days I'm going to give you what for. I was sure I was going to find you up to your neck in quicksand."

"One of these days, Peg, you're going to stop worrying so much," replied Wally. "Anyway, there's your island. What do you think?"

"It looks huge!" said Wiru, as she and the rest of the wallabies emerged from the swamp.

The island rose out of the river as a sheer rock wall that towered above them, stretching into the distance downstream. The wall was almost vertical, far too steep to climb, and polished at the base by years of running water.

"We'd better take a closer look at that causeway," said Wally. "That looks like the only way across."

The path through the swamp had delivered the wallabies to a small patch of soggy ground. They had to struggle up a mound of moss and mud that led to the causeway. Finding a footing on the slippery slope was difficult, and by the time they reached the top, they were covered in mud and slime.

From the summit of the mound, they could see the island divided the river, with most of the water flowing on the far side. The remainder ran on the swamp side, where the bulk of it flowed over the causeway. The rest drained into the swamp.

The causeway was a pile of rocks that bridged the river between the swamp and the island, formed when part of the wall had cracked and collapsed into the water. Some of the rocks jutted above the surface, breaking the river's flow, but other sections of the causeway were underwater. The group would need to use the submerged rocks to brace themselves against the current. Even though most of the river ran on the other side of the island, the current over the shallow causeway was still strong.

On the far side, a small landing was visible below the crack in the rock wall. Through the crack, a narrow path led into the island, as though leading into the heart of the massive stone wall. The causeway was the only way onto the island from the swamp, and if you slipped and fell in, there would be no way to get out. You'd be at the mercy of the river.

"I have to say," said Jake wistfully, "I'm getting tired of these river crossings."

"Hopefully, this will be the last crossing for a while," said Peg, surveying the causeway, trying to determine the best way to approach it.

"Who's going first this time?" asked Ned.

"I'll go," said Wiru. "It's probably not as dangerous as it looks."

"Just be careful," warned Ned. "Remember what the ram said. The rocks will probably be slippery."

Wiru made her way easily over the first half of the causeway, bouncing across the exposed rocks, until she confronted the flowing water. She dipped a foot in to test the current. Steadying herself with her front paws, she edged out into the stream. Taking small, careful steps, she moved slowly between and over the smooth, submerged rocks, eventually making her way to the other side.

"Come on, it's not too bad!" she called. "Just take small steps!"

One by one, the wallabies took their turn. But when Wally readied himself for the crossing, he found he could barely move. Memories of his previous ordeal in the river played with his mind and stiffened his limbs. It was too late to turn back, so he forced himself forward, trying not to show his fear.

He bounced awkwardly over the dry rocks until he was face to face with the swift current. As he stepped into the water, his fear surged.

"Come on!" he told himself. "If the others can cross, it can't be that hard."

He moved carefully into the water, his fear rising as his body sank lower into the stream. The noise of the water racing over the causeway was unnerving, but he pushed himself forward, clinging to whatever support he could find.

"Slowly, slowly," he thought as his feet slid over the slippery stones.

With each small step, his confidence grew until finally his feet found the small bank on the other side. He leapt up onto the landing, the relief flooding over him.

Soon, all the wallabies had crossed, with Ned coming over last.

They stood on the small bank above the causeway, peering into the crack in the cliff. The path beyond was so dense with foliage it was more like a tunnel. Long, thin vines hung down from above, filled with spiders that had spun their webs between the vines, like hundreds of little fishermen, trying to catch their daily meal. Thick ferns covered the ground, growing across the path as if trying to conceal it. What little light found its way into the crack diminished in the depths of the tunnel.

The wallabies stared into the passage, scarcely believing that this was the path forward. Everything the ram had said had checked out, the path through the swamp, the log, the causeway, but he hadn't mentioned this.

"Looks like that's the only way to go," said Ned, nodding towards the path. "Let's see where it takes us."

He hopped cautiously into the opening. The girls followed, leaving Wally and Jake alone on the landing.

"So far, so good," said Jake, noticing Wally's hesitation. "Are you okay?"

"Yeah, I'm fine," said Wally, watching the others disappear into the tunnel. "Just giving Ned a chance to clear the cobwebs."

Wally paused, troubled by something. "Hey Jake," he said, "have I got crazy ears?"

"What?"

"Are my ears uneven?"

"Yeah. One's much bigger than the other."

"What? Why didn't you tell me?"

"I thought you knew."

"How on earth would I know? They don't feel different."

Wally shook his head, as if that might fix them, but they felt no different than before.

"Well, come on," said Jake, slightly confused. "We'd better go. We don't want to lose the others."

They turned, twisted, and squeezed through the crack. By the time they reached the end, Ned had thick cobwebs stretched across his ears. Through the trees, they saw a huge clearing, a warm welcome into a rich, open land. The island was much longer than it had appeared from the swamp, covered in thick grass and trees. Dozens of wallabies of all kinds lay in the sun, while their joeys played nearby.

"Wow!" exclaimed Peg, hopping into the clearing. "And I thought Rocky Hill was special! Look at this!"

As the mob tried to take it all in, two rock wallabies approached.

"Looks like we have a welcoming party," said Jake.

"Hello!" said one. "Welcome to the island. It's been a long time since we've had any guests."

"And judging by the mud on your fur, that swamp hasn't dried up yet," said the other. "How did you find your way through there?"

"We came across a ram named Blue Belly Joe. He gave us directions," replied Ned.

"Really? And you still managed to find your way through?" the wallaby asked, a smile widening across his face. "That ram is a nice enough bloke, but he's a complete nutter. I've got no idea how he remembers the route through the swamp."

"Or how often he gets it right!" said the first. "Looks like it's your lucky day!"

The two wallabies laughed, but the group were horrified that the ram's directions might have been completely wrong.

"Anyway, I'm glad you all made it," said the first wallaby. "Come on, we'll show you around."

The guides led them through the bush to a lookout on the crest of the cliff, far above the plain. From there, the island resembled a long, giant egg with most of the centre carved out. The rock wall rose up on the north side of the island, but inside the wall a vast open plain spread to the southern edge, covered in lush, green grass and fringed by trees and shrubs. The plains extended almost halfway to the eastern side. On the cliff to the east, a grassy shelf jutted out. Rock wallabies peppered the eastern ledges, soaking up the afternoon sun.

Wally looked to the north. The ram had been right, they would have had a long and difficult journey around the swamp, which stretched as far as he could see, bordered by dense, tangled bush. He could see the causeway and the muddy mound before it, but the track through the swamp was invisible from above. All he could see was a sea of reeds, waving gently in the breeze.

"Do you see that shelf over on the other side of the wall?" asked one of the guides, pointing with his paw. "There's a little waterhole up there called Platypus Pool. Sometimes you can see platypuses playing in there. There's a big gathering up there tonight. Everyone will be going, you should come along?"

"We'd love to," said Peg, sparkling at the hospitality.

"Great. And if you want a swim, the swimming hole is over there," he added, pointing to a small rocky hook that extended into the river on the southern side of the island.

"Feel free to look around. There's plenty to see. We'll see you tonight at Platypus Pool."

The two rock wallabies turned and disappeared down the trail.

"No offence," said Peg, turning to the Rocky Hill wallabies, "but that's a far better welcome than the one we got at Rocky Hill. I love this place already. Who wants to go down to the swimming hole and wash some of this mud off?"

Everyone was keen to go, except Wally.

"I think I'll hang around here for a while and see if I can climb to the top of this rock. How about we meet back at the start of the clearing at sunset, and head to the gathering together?"

"Sounds great," said Peg. "Have fun. We'll see you soon."

Once the others had gone, Wally made his way through the bush to the top of the rock wall. The crest was narrow, barely wide enough for a single wallaby, but from there he could see the entire island. He looked into the distance, hoping to see some sign of the ocean, even though he wasn't sure what he was looking for. But all he could see was the river, winding deeper into the landscape.

"How much farther did he have to go?" he wondered. They'd been travelling for days, and the end of the river was still nowhere in sight.

He looked down at the expanse of open land below him and spotted the small bay that must have been the swimming hole. Then he saw his mob, far off in the distance, hopping towards the bay. A pang of loneliness passed through him.

He could feel his influence on the group waning. He already sensed some resistance to the plan of reaching the ocean. He could understand why, after all, the ocean was his dream. To most wallabies, the island was ideal. Once again, he realised if he left, it was unlikely they'd all want to follow, if indeed any of them would.

He traced the river as it turned sharply at the end of the island and then, a long way in the distance, he saw it turn back on itself, forming a giant open loop. At the end of the loop, it turned back again into bushland and disappeared.

* * *

When Wally returned to the clearing, he found Jake lying in the shade of a gum tree, trying to catch a wink of sleep.

"So, you've completed your reconnaissance of the island and are now resting?" he asked.

"Correct," replied Jake, barely opening an eye. "We are on an island, and there is a big field in front of us. Mission accomplished."

"Did you go down for a swim with the others?"

"Not yet. I might go down there later this afternoon, but I thought I'd just have a moment of peace and quiet first. There's plenty of time for exploring."

"Yep, I get that," said Wally. "It's quite a place, isn't it?"

"It sure is," said Jake. "I would never have believed it existed if I hadn't seen it with my own eyes. Definitely worth traipsing through that swamp, don't you think?"

Wally lay down in the shade alongside Jake and looked out over the field. Without any trouble at all, he counted seven different types of wallabies.

"Yes," he said. "Definitely worth traipsing through that swamp."

TADPOLES

Late that afternoon, the wallabies regrouped at the edge of the clearing and made their way across the open field and up to Platypus Pool. As they climbed the narrow track that led to the pool, the sounds of conversation and laughter grew louder. At the top of the path, they found a flat, spacious landing on the side of the escarpment, thick with grass and dotted with large boulders. Just a stone's throw beyond was Platypus Pool, nestled behind the rocks along the side of the cliff.

The landing was teeming with wallabies of many kinds and colours, black stripes and red necks, whiptails and brushtails, rocks and swamps, and even a few wallabies that Wally had never seen before.

Ned led the little mob into the crowd and found a small patch of grass just big enough for the group. Just as they began to settle in, one of the elder wallabies stood up and began to speak.

"Welcome, one and all, young and old, big and small, to the monthly Kanandah Bash. And a special welcome to the group of wallabies who arrived earlier today," the announcer declared, tipping his head toward Wally's mob. "And now to the matters at hand…"

After some formalities, announcements, and praise for some of the younger wallabies' feats of skill, the crowd dispersed to talk while the joeys played games in the soft grass. Wally's mob mingled in the crowd, learning all they could about the island. By all accounts, it was a wallaby paradise. Food and water were plentiful, and, as they had hoped, almost completely free of predators. Even the eagles didn't bother with the island; they could be seen easily from a long way off, giving the wallabies ample time to raise the alarm and find shelter.

Time passed quickly, and twilight began to descend on the gathering, as the full moon grew brighter in the sky. The elder stood up and once again requested the attention of the audience.

"All right, everyone, it's story time! Is there anyone who would like to share a story with us tonight or shall we just get Uncle Bob to tell the story of the Possum and the Butterfly again?"

A great murmur of discontent ran through the crowd.

"Please! No! Not again!" someone shouted. "Not the Possum and the Butterfly!"

"Yes, anything but that! I'd rather listen to the cicadas!" cried another.

"Well, if no one else has a story to tell…" the

elder continued.

"Jake has a story!" Peg called out mischievously, putting Jake on the spot.

"Peg!" Jake replied harshly, although secretly he relished the chance to tell his story again.

"Come on then, Jake," said the elder. "Share your story with us."

Jake stood and walked to the front of the assembly. He cleared his throat and began the tale.

"In a land beyond the western horizon, where nothing grew but discontent, there lived a small mob of wallabies, struggling to survive. Every day, a scorching sun beat down on them so fiercely that it almost singed the fur on their backs. Barely a blade of grass grew in all of that unforgiving land, and the only water came from the tears that fell from the wallabies' eyes. They were ruled by a harsh and cranky old commander who refused to move them on until one day, one of the wallabies said, 'Enough'."

Peg leaned over and nudged Wally. "This story gets better every time he tells it. I can't wait till he gets to the part about the crocodile."

"He's talking about us, right?" Wally asked as Jake went on. "There's a fair bit of this story I don't seem to remember."

Peg giggled. "He's very good at telling it though, isn't he? Look at the crowd."

Wally looked around, and it was true. Jake had them spellbound, as each part of the story grew larger than life.

"Yes, he does," Wally said with a smile. He listened for a while longer and then turned to Peg. "Well, I know how this one ends. I'm going over to the pool for a drink."

He got to his feet quietly, but no one paid him any mind, the eyes of the crowd were all focused on Jake.

Wally made his way to the pool, the moon just strong enough to glisten on the water's surface. He looked down and saw his reflection staring back, as the tiniest ripples in the pond distorted his features.

"Some great leader you turned out to be," he said. "You can barely keep a handful of wallabies together, let alone a mob. Really. You can't even hop in a straight line."

He started to think about who he was, what he was doing, his responsibility to Jake and Peg, and now the rest of the band of wallabies. Suddenly a thousand questions sparked in his mind. What was it that made him feel responsible for the other wallabies? What was this trip all about? Why was it so important that he travel to the ocean? What did he expect to find? How could he turn his back on the island paradise to look for something when he didn't even know what it was? How did that make any sense? And why did he feel it was so necessary that they all got there? Why was it so important to him that the band stayed together? Why did he feel like he had to be the leader? Was that just something he'd gotten used to because he felt responsible for Jake and Peg when they left their mob? Or was he just being selfish because he wanted to control the direction of the journey? The Rocky Hill wallabies weren't even from his old mob, why did he care about them?

Then he noticed his ears. "My ears *are* uneven," he thought. "What *else* is wrong with me?"

He looked deeply into his reflection in the pool, lost in his thoughts, digging himself deeper and deeper into the hole of his own misery just as the sounds of laughter erupted from Jake's tale, almost as though the whole crowd was mocking him.

"What are you looking at?"

The voice startled Wally. He turned quickly to find Wiru standing a few hops behind him.

"Ah, nothing," he said, caught completely off guard and embarrassed by his self-indulgence. "Just some tadpoles," he replied, making up a story to cover his thoughts. "Can you see them? There were plenty here a second ago, they must have all just swum off."

"Tadpoles? Bit odd to come out here looking for tadpoles at this time of night, isn't it? Why aren't you listening to Jake? It's a great story, especially the way he tells it."

"I know how that one goes," he said flatly. "I guess I was hoping to see a platypus or something." He wished he had thought of that earlier. Tadpoles? Why would he be looking for tadpoles in a pond called Platypus Pool?

"You want to be careful about staring into pools, Wally, you never know what might be staring back." She smiled. "How's the knee?"

"Same as ever, I suppose. Maybe a little better, but it's hard to say. It was pretty slow going through that scrub before the swamp. I haven't really had a chance to test it in the open, but there hasn't been any misfires for a while, so I guess that's something."

"How long have you had the problem with your knee?"

"Since I was a joey. I was born with it."

Wiru began to smile.

"Okay, go ahead and laugh. It is pretty funny, I suppose. A wallaby with a wobbly knee. What kind of a wallaby gets around with a wobbly knee?"

"I was smiling because I think I understand now. I was wondering why Jake and Peg look up to you so much. I mean, you're not exactly a big and powerful wallaby."

"I doubt they look up to me as much as you

think."

"You're wrong, Wally. They think the world of you. They might not say as much to your face, but it's obvious from an outsider's perspective. All of us can see it. It was there the moment you walked into Rocky Hill. You should go and listen to how Jake describes you in his story."

"Come on. I know Jake."

"It's true. You seem to think of that knee as a weakness, but your knee is what made you who you are."

Wally turned and looked at Wiru, puzzled. "What?"

"Where do you think you get your determination and your spirit? Since you were a joey, you've had to deal with something that most other wallabies never have to even think about. A wallaby with an unreliable knee, I can't imagine how difficult that must have been, how different you must have felt. But it didn't stop you, did it? According to Jake, you were going to leave your mob on your own. With a wobbly knee! Where do you think that kind of courage comes from?"

"Courage or craziness?"

"Can you have one without the other? I'm sure you take it for granted now but think about what you've done. None of us would be here if it wasn't for you. That knee has shaped you, Wally. It's a part of everything about you. It's made you, well, you."

Wally's gaze never left Wiru. Finally, Wiru looked away, fearing she may have said too much.

"Anyway, I just came up here to make sure you were okay. You seemed a little, I don't know, detached today. I'll see you back at the gathering, okay?"

She turned and made her way back to the rest of the wallabies, leaving Wally alone at the edge of the pool.

Suddenly, as though Wiru's words had shattered a great weight that had been sitting on his shoulders, Wally realised his responsibility was to himself. He hadn't started this journey to become a leader of a mob or to assume responsibility for a bunch of wallabies that happened to want to join him. He had felt responsible for Jake and Peg because leaving the mob had been his idea. Then again, when the Rocky Hill wallabies joined, he felt responsible for them. But all that had really happened was that a bunch of wallabies felt the same way he did and had joined his journey.

His journey.

Though they had all been travelling together, each wallaby had their own path, and each would decide where that path would lead and where it would end. If the others had found a place where they were happy, well, he would be happy for them. But he still needed to finish his journey, alone, if need be.

And what difference did it make if he had two odd ears and a wobbly knee? Wiru was right. That was just him, and all him, at exactly the same time.

He looked back into the pool, expecting to see his uneven ears waving back.

But this time, all he saw were tadpoles.

Simple Words

By morning, Wally had made his plans for departure. There was no rush; he would take the day to say his farewells and leave the following morning. He hopped out into the open field and started to casually leap along the boundary. Almost unconsciously, his pace quickened, and before he knew it, he was bounding at full speed. It had been a while since he'd run through an open field, and even though he was restricted by the size of the island, it felt good. It felt like him again.

After a couple of laps, he paused on the south side of the island and looked out once more at the river that was guiding his life. He began thinking about his departure, the travel back across the causeway, through the swamp, and finding the long way around to get back on track. This had been a long detour, but a good one all the same, especially for the rest of the mob.

He turned to head back and saw two young joeys standing behind him.

"Excuse me, mister. You're Wally, aren't

you?" one of them asked.

"Yes," Wally replied. "How did you know my name?"

"You're famous."

"What are you talking about?"

"From the story last night. Jake said you saved his life, and Peg's life too."

"Don't go believing everything you hear," Wally replied. "Especially from Jake."

Embarrassed by his sudden fame, Wally changed the subject. "It certainly is a beautiful island you have here. Have you two been here long?"

"We were born here. Are you going to stay, Mister Wally?"

"I'd like to, but I can't. I need to go and find the ocean."

"Is it lost?"

"No, it's at the end of the river, wherever that is."

"I didn't even know the river had an end," said the second joey. "We've never been off the island."

"When are you going to leave?" asked the first joey.

"Tomorrow morning. And I have to say, I'm not looking forward to going back through that swamp."

"But if you're going down the river, why don't you just swim across from the swimming hole? That's what everyone else does."

"What?" asked Wally. "What do they do?"

"They go down to the swimming hole, walk into the river, and start swimming. The current carries you downstream, but the first bend is quite sharp, so it swings you over to the far side and you just walk out from there."

"I see," said Wally. "I might go and take a closer look at that swimming hole."

"Are you sure you have to go?" asked the second joey.

"I'm afraid I do. But I want to thank you both. I didn't know you could cross the river that way. You might have just saved me two or three days of travel."

"We helped Wally!" said the first joey to the second. "Let's go and tell the others. Thanks, Mister Wally. Good luck!"

The joeys bounded away, thrilled by the thought they had helped the character from Jake's story, while Wally wondered just how far Jake had gone. He turned and made his way towards the swimming hole.

The swimming hole had formed behind a long finger of stone that curved out from the island and into the river's flow. Inside the curve, the water was protected, forming a pool of still water adjacent to the fast-flowing current.

When Wally arrived, he could see exactly what the joeys had described. At the end of the island, the river turned sharply, he'd seen as much from the lookout, leaving a shallow overflow on the far bank. If he could swim across and let the current carry him, he could easily exit at the bend. Then he could cut even more time off the journey by travelling across the grassland and meeting the river further downstream, bypassing the river's wide loop.

He walked out along the rocky finger to the river's edge and watched the water rush past. "So much water," he thought. "Moving so quickly." He wondered where it was all going and why it was in such a hurry to get there. He watched leaves falling into the river, racing in the current, and realised that, like them, he too would soon become a passenger of the river's flow.

He returned to the swimming hole and waded into the cool water as the cicadas buzzed in the river gums along the shore. The refreshing water washed the mud from his fur and cleared the worry from his mind. By crossing the river again, it felt like all the troubles that had been chasing him would disappear, the dingoes, the wild dogs, the Rocky Hill mob. He couldn't have known that by then, there was nothing left to worry about anyway.

He gave himself to the water, swimming lazily in the shadow of the gums. When he finally emerged, he felt relaxed and happy. The next leg of the journey was all set. All that he had to do now were the farewells.

Back at the clearing, on the patch of grass his mob had begun to call home, he found only Ned lying peacefully in the sun.

"G'day, Ned. I'm looking for Peg. Have you seen her?"

"Yes, she and the girls went up to Platypus Pool. Wiru had some crazy idea about going looking for tadpoles or something. They left a little while ago."

Wally smiled. "Okay, thanks. I'll go and see if they're still up there."

He turned and bounded across the open field, his knee feeling stronger as he gathered pace. At Platypus Pool, he found Peg and Agnes lying in the shade while Wiru and Ellin played in the rocks beside the pool.

"You two look comfortable," he said as he approached.

"Ah, the wandering hero," Peg teased. "To what do we owe this honour?"

"Very funny. I think I'd better have a talk with Jake about that." He paused, struggling to find a way to say what he had to say, and decided to just get it out. "I just came up to say goodbye. I'm leaving in the morning."

"What? Goodbye?"

Peg looked at Wally and saw the look in his eyes. "Oh no. Wally, no! How can you even think of going on? This is everything we wanted. Everything. It's the reason we left our mob. We've done it, Wally. We've found what we were looking for."

"Peg, I'm really happy you feel that way, but I'm not finished. I have to get to the ocean. I have to see it now."

"Who cares about the stupid ocean, Wally? You don't even know what it is! Stop and look at where we are. This is it, Wally! It's perfect! The pools, the fields, food, water, even the other wallabies are great. We've found it. After all that distance, we've finally found it! This is home!"

"Not for me, Peg. And you're right, I don't know what's at the ocean, but I have to find out. I don't even know why. I just do."

"Oh, Wally, how far is far enough? When we came out here, we came because we were starving. Well, we're not starving anymore. Look what you are turning your back on. What on earth are you running to?"

Wally just looked at her, knowing what was coming.

"Look, Wally, you led us out of that barren land, through the Divide, and away from that horrible mob. But this is enough for me. More than enough. I can't go any further, Wally. I just can't."

Though he was prepared for it, Wally still felt the thump in his chest.

"I know," he said quietly.

"Think about what you're doing, Wally. You'll regret..."

"Peg," he interrupted gently. "I'll miss you."

"Oh, you'll forget me before you're over the next hill." She turned away so he wouldn't see the tears welling in her eyes.

"Come on, Peg. How could I possibly forget you? This journey wouldn't have been the same without you."

"You didn't even invite me along. If Jake hadn't told me you were going, I'd still be back in that hopeless mob, probably starved to death." She reflected on the journey, all the challenges and all the triumphs. "God, we've come a long way."

"It doesn't matter if I invited you or not, Peg. What matters is how much better the journey was with you. I really will miss you."

"I'll miss your knee, Wally, and your stupid flying tricks."

"You can have my knee..."

Peg smiled and looked at him, with his uneven ears and his messed-up knee. She hopped over and gave him a hug. Their eyes met for a moment, and in that moment, said all the things that were never meant for simple words.

* * *

It was late afternoon before Wally finally found Jake.

"Hey, Jake."

"Wally. How's it going?"

"Good. Listen, mate, I came to say goodbye. I'm leaving in the morning."

"I know."

"You know?"

"Peg told me. Though I can't say it was really news. I figured you were going to leave, sooner or later."

"Look, I can't really explain why. I just need to finish what I started. I have to get to the ocean."

"Yep. I know. You're one of those wallabies who gets an idea in his head and has to see it through, otherwise you'd go crazy wondering what might have been."

"Yes, something like that." It wasn't the reaction Wally had been expecting at all.

"So, when are we leaving?"

"What?"

"You don't think I'm just going to sit around here all day and watch the sun move, do you? What's the use of a storyteller if he doesn't have a story to tell? Let the adventure continue, I say."

Wally was stunned. He hadn't expected Jake would want to go with him, but his heart lifted at the thought. "I was thinking tomorrow morning, early."

"Please don't say 'first light'. Remember that? You sounded like some kind of drill sergeant. What's the rush anyway? A few people will want to see us off, why don't we make it mid-morning, instead of trying to sneak off at the crack of dawn."

"Okay, sure."

"It's going to feel weird without Peg."

"Yes, it will."

"She said she felt like she was letting you down by not going."

"That's crazy. She's not letting me down. I've been lucky to have you both along."

"That's true."

"Probably. Except for you. You know, you got your tail infected. That was a hassle. Slowed us right down. Then you walked me into the un-crossable river..."

"...that Peg and I crossed..."

"...and then led us straight into the Rocky Hill mob..."

"Oh, that..."

"Yep. I'm so glad you're coming with me."

"I wouldn't want to disappoint you."

"Great."

They both smiled, knowing they had successfully not said anything they had really wanted to say, yet had somehow managed to convey the sentiment.

"I don't suppose you've seen Darcy, have you?"

"He's gone. Took off before we settled down on the first night. I saw him run into the trees and join a group of sugar gliders. I doubt you'll find him. He came back this morning beaming about some amazing acrobatic flight, and all the fun he was having with the other gliders. Peg said he took his owl feathers with him."

By late evening, everyone in the little mob knew that Wally and Jake were leaving, except Darcy. No one could find him, no matter where they looked. Wally was about to head into the trees again to look for him when Wiru approached.

"Hi, Wiru."

"Hi. Look, I just stopped by to tell you I'll be coming with you, and I won't be taking 'no' for an answer."

"Okay. Are you sure?" Wally asked, surprised but delighted. He thought all the Rocky Hill wallabies wanted to stay.

"Absolutely. What time do we leave?"

"Tomorrow morning."

"First light?"

Wally laughed. "Yes. Tell Jake."

And then he laughed even harder.

SAILORS

The Wooden Eagle crashed its way through the next set of rapids with barely any trouble, carrying the two devils further down the river. The days on the raft had passed quickly as they took turns steering it downstream, but their last meal was now a distant memory, and both devils' bellies were rumbling.

Horatio knew it was impossible to believe they were actually heading towards Tasmania, but he didn't have the heart to shatter Bongo's fantasy. Bongo seemed convinced they were on the right path, and really, what was the harm in that? Sooner or later, Bongo would realise, and the later the better. With a purpose in mind, Bongo had become a completely different individual.

"How long do you think it will be before we get to Tasmania?" Horatio asked. "I'm starting to get hungry."

"There's still a way to go yet," replied Bongo, looking out over the bow as though Tasmania would somehow loom out of the river. "I'm getting a bit hungry too. Just a little way further and then maybe we should..."

Suddenly, as they rounded another long bend, a huge island appeared in the middle of the river. For a moment, Bongo was convinced they had found Tasmania, but his hopes were quickly dashed when he realised it was far too small.

"For a moment there, I thought we were home," he said. "But that's not Tasmania. We must be getting closer though. I bet the next island we come across will be Tassie."

"I'm sure it will be," said Horatio.

*   *   *

A large crowd had gathered around the swimming hole that morning to farewell the three wallabies. The trio hopped out along the rocky pier to the point where they would enter the river.

"I take it this crowd is your doing?" Wally said to Jake.

"I've got no idea what you're talking about," Jake replied, smiling. "What can I say? You're a popular guy, Wally."

Wally just shook his head.

"Alright," he said, "I think we're good to go. The plan is to jump off that big rock over there, as far out into the river as you can. The river looks to be flowing pretty fast, so let's not waste any time swimming across, okay? I really don't want a repeat of my last trip down the river."

Jake and Wiru nodded. Wally prepared to jump when he noticed an unusual object coming down the river.

"Hey Hozza," Bongo asked, seeing the three wallabies on the rocks at the edge of the island. "Isn't that the kangaroo we met way back in the desert?"

"How many times am I going to have to tell you this? That wasn't a kangaroo, it was a wallaby. And technically, it wasn't a desert, just a very dry grassland. And yes, that appears to be him. But what are the chances our paths would cross again? Pretty small, I'd say. It's probably just a wallaby that looks like him. They all look a bit the same, don't you think?"

"What was his name again? Henry or Harry or Jelly or something, wasn't it?"

"I think it was Wally. But that was quite some time ago."

"Yes, Wally! That sounds right. Let's find out if it's him."

"Hey, Wally!" Bongo shouted as they drifted past. "How's it going?"

Every head on the island suddenly turned toward the two Tasmanian devils, sailing casually down the river on The Wooden Eagle. Then they looked at Wally.

"He's got ferocious-looking animals for

friends!" someone shouted.

The crowd cheered wildly.

Wally watched in disbelief as the devils sailed past. "Well, I'll be blowed," he said, raising a paw to wave.

"Friends of yours?" asked Jake.

"Sort of. Acquaintances, really. I met them on the other side of the Divide."

"They're pretty good sailors, aren't they?" Jake remarked.

"Doesn't that strike you as strange?" Wally asked.

"Not really. Maybe all those animals are good sailors."

"No. I mean that they found a way across the Divide."

"Well, now that you mention it. But watching them float down the river like that, do you ever get the feeling we do everything the hard way? Look, they're nearly around the bend already."

"How on earth did they get through the Divide?" Wally wondered. Was there something he didn't know? Some secret passage that he'd missed? Maybe there was a whole ark full of animals coming through the Divide.

Just then, something slammed into Wally's back, nearly knocking him off his feet. He stumbled as the claws dug into his skin, then ran up onto his shoulder. It was Darcy, flying in to say goodbye.

As Wally regained his balance, Darcy punched his tiny fist in the air and yelled to the crowd, "Wally!"

And the crowd roared back.

"Nice of you to make an entrance," Wally said, looking at the sugar glider perched on his shoulder.

"Well, I wasn't going to let you leave without saying goodbye."

"It's good to see you, Darcy. Jake said you've found some mates."

"Oh yeah, they're awesome. They're showing me flying tricks I'd never even heard of. I love it here, and there's so much to eat!" he said greedily.

"Look after Peg for us, won't you?" Wally said as he set Darcy down on the nearest tree, gently touching the soft fur on his head.

"No worries. Wally," Darcy paused. "And Wally, good luck."

Wally smiled, just as a chant rose up from the crowd.

"Wally! Wally!"

"What on earth did you tell them the other night?" he asked Jake.

"Nothing. Just our story. Honest."

"Yeah, right."

"Well, if we're going to go, how about a little showmanship?"

"Like what?" Wally asked.

"Like one of your signature backflips."

Wally smiled at the thought. "You really love to ham it up, don't you?"

With that, he turned, took two strong leaps, and threw himself off the big rock, executing a perfect backflip before splashing into the river.

The current picked him up immediately, as he swam towards the surface.

The island fell silent as Wally disappeared into the water. The moment his head broke the surface, another huge roar erupted from the crowd.

"Nice one, mate," Jake called as he turned to Wiru. "Shall we?"

"Of course," she said as she and Jake bounded out and hurled themselves into the river, Jake making as big a splash as he could, to the delight of the crowd.

The river had the wallabies then, and they began their long swim across the current.

Wally made the distance easily and was near the far bank when the river finally turned and swung him to the shore. He glanced back to see Wiru and Jake close behind.

Wading out of the water, he shook himself dry, and looked back upstream. He saw the wallabies on the island waving just as Jake and Wiru emerged from the river. The three stood and waved back, then scampered up the bank and out into the open field.

THE WORLD OF PAYNE

Well beyond the bend at the end of the island, the devils encountered the final stretch of rapids. Mild in comparison to what they had faced upstream, the roughened water felt more like a farewell, as though the river was signalling the end of the carriage of the little raft before finally finding its level. Horatio navigated the log as it accelerated through the quickening water, before it was thrust out into the middle of the widening river.

They had no idea how far the river had carried them, but now, as the raft began to drift slowly and aimlessly down the waterway, it was clearly time to return to solid ground.

"Bongo, I'm starving. We haven't eaten in days. I think we should beach the raft and go find something to eat. It will be faster to walk now; the river has slowed to little more than a standstill."

"Sounds good. I'm really hungry too."

"Which side of the river would you prefer?"

Bongo looked out over the front of the log and surveyed the banks. The land beyond the left bank was flat and grassy, framed by a large escarpment that rose sharply from the plain. On the right, green rolling hills stretched as far as the eye could see.

"I'm not sure," he said. "Either side looks okay, but neither side looks anything like Tasmania. I would have thought if we were getting closer, things would start to look more like home."

"Seems logical enough," said Horatio. He knew it didn't matter which side they landed on, just that they got back to solid ground.

"On the one hand," Bongo continued, "those cliffs look appealing, lots of shade, probably caves and rocks, but they kind of cut the land off."

"Yes."

"But those hills on the right look like they go on forever. Which is great but also a bit boring."

"That's true too. So which side do you think?"

"I'm not sure. Neither looks right."

"Well, we have to find something to eat."

"Hmmm."

Horatio could almost see the cogs turning in Bongo's head. It had already been a long day on The Wooden Eagle, and Horatio was sure he'd done more than his share of the steering. He was hungry and tired, and the last thing he wanted was another long debate.

"I'll tell you what," he said. "Why don't you have a good think about it and wake me up when you've decided?" He handed the paddle to Bongo and moved up to the front of the raft. He lay down, leaving the raft to drift gently in the middle of the river.

"On the other hand..." Bongo began, finding yet another feature to consider.

As soon as Horatio lay down, he realised how tired he was. They had been on the river for days, without much sleep, making sure the raft stayed on course, constantly keeping watch for rough water. It only took a moment after he closed his eyes for sleep to take him.

An hour later, with the raft still drifting slowly, Bongo still hadn't made up his mind.

"How do you choose something if it's not really what you want?" he thought.

Finally, the tiredness and the mental struggle with the decision got the better of him. He curled up alongside Horatio. With the water lapping gently at the side of the log, he went straight to sleep, leaving it to the river to decide.

In the early hours of the following morning, The Wooden Eagle beached itself with a gentle nudge on a small sandy beach on the right-hand side of the river. The beach was advertised widely as yet another idyllic feature of a small resort run by Rex and Sharon Payne, called the World of Payne Tent and Caravan Park, located in the middle of almost nowhere on the eastern coast of Australia. A well-worn, windy track, a few hundred metres long, connected the beach to the resort.

When Horatio woke, the sun was already high in the sky, filtered through the leaves of a large jacaranda. He looked over the side of the raft, surprised, happy, and relieved that Bongo had beached the raft while he slept. He wondered how long it had taken Bongo to do it, considering the river was now barely moving. He couldn't have had much sleep. As he looked around at the beach and the bank, he had to give Bongo credit, he had picked a very pleasant location to end their journey down the river.

He began to wonder how long he could continue with the charade that they were actually on their way back to Tasmania. He still had no doubt the task was impossible, but the idea that they were on their way home made Bongo feel better. He looked down at him, curled up peacefully in the bottom of the log, and thought twice about letting him sleep in, but his hunger got the better of him.

He shook Bongo gently until Bongo's eyes finally opened.

"Good job with the raft, mate. Now let's go and find something to eat."

Despite the distance, the smell of breakfast cooking at the caravan park wafted down to the river that day, and the aroma was irresistible to the hungry devils. Abandoning The Wooden Eagle, they made their way hurriedly along the trail, running headlong toward the World of Payne.

THOSE NAGGING FEARS

Once the wallabies had cleared the bank, they found themselves on an open field that separated them from the thick bush in the distance.

"From what I could see from the lookout on the island," Wally explained, "the river heads to the left and then loops all the way back to a point somewhere over there," he said, pointing to the right. "We should be able to cut through this plain and save ourselves a day or two."

"I like the sound of that," said Jake. "Might as well get started then. I'll race you to that stump!" he called, already a good five hops in front.

The wallabies chased each other through the field, making easy progress on the grassy terrain. By nightfall, they had reached the other side of the loop and found that the whole river had changed. The water was now still, and the river had widened considerably. Wally could hardly believe it was the same river that had once hurled him through the rapids so violently above the waterfall. He wondered if it was a sign that they were getting closer.

"I guess we just follow it from here," said Wally, "but that can wait until tomorrow. I'm beat."

"You must be getting old, Wally. I'm fine," teased Wiru.

"Maybe," he replied, "but it probably has more to do with the extra weight of my swelled head since Jake's been telling everyone what a hero I am."

"Your head does look a bit bigger, mate," Jake retorted, "but it still hasn't fixed your ears."

"Oh, maybe a little," said Wiru, smiling.

"Very funny," said Wally, settling into the riverbank.

It had been a good day; they'd made a lot of progress, and his knee hadn't misfired once. He felt like he was back on track, happy to be out in the open again, and better still, had the company of two companions. He understood Jake's reasons for coming, but he wasn't so sure about Wiru.

"Wiru," he asked as the night fell, "what made you want to come with us? That island seemed perfect. No dingoes, plenty of food and water, it had everything."

"Except movement," she replied without having to think about it. "I could just see everyone getting so complacent on that island they'd never leave. And if they did, their senses would be so dull they wouldn't last long. It reminded me of the early days at Rocky Hill, before the dogs arrived." She thought for a moment. "Besides, I want more than that. I want to see what's out there. I want some of that adventure Jake keeps talking about, and I want to experience it, not just hear about it."

"I hope I haven't talked you into something that may not live up to your expectations," said Jake.

"Come on, Jake," she said, "I know how you tell stories, but there's a thread of truth in every one. Given the choice between lying around in safety or the experience of adventure, I'll take the adventure any day. Mind you, I would've been happy to relax on that island for a few more days, but I knew that if I didn't go with you, I'd never convince anyone else to leave. Agnes was already calling it home. Besides, this ocean place sounds exciting. Mysterious, even. Like a journey into the unknown."

"It's definitely that," said Wally. "I've got no idea what to expect."

"That's part of what makes it so appealing. It's thrilling and frightening being out here, just the three of us. I've got no idea how you could even think of doing that on your own, Wally. I couldn't have done that, it's like you have no fear."

"I have fear," said Jake. "I think I've got enough fear for all three of us."

"Don't worry, I have those fears too," said Wally. "Those nagging fears. But if you don't face them, you'll carry them for the rest of your life." He looked over to Wiru. "And they get pretty heavy."

"So he faced the commander, and the dingoes, and the crocodiles, goannas, fires, rivers, a loopy mob, and a swamp, and dragged poor Peg and me through it all with him," joked Jake.

"They were pretty heavy too." Wally smiled, and Wiru smiled back. He was glad she had decided to come.

Sleep found the wallabies easily that night. They couldn't have known, but by the afternoon of the next day, they would be standing on a beach.

MULLOWAY

It was the worst surfing trip in living memory. At least, that's how Terry would tell the story. Ten days driving up the east coast of Australia with barely a wave to show for it. Terry had spent weeks prior to departure researching weather patterns, swell forecasts, and tides, even the geography of the headlands, in an attempt to predict where and when he could expect optimum surfing conditions. But if the absence of waves was the measure, Terry had timed his holiday to perfection. The ocean had been like a lake the entire time.

His dreams of recreating the photos from his surfing magazines now lay discarded on the floor of the Ford Fairlane, alongside fast-food wrappers and half-empty tubes of sunblock. Without waves, Terry and his girlfriend, Lorraine, had spent most of their time reading and sunbaking in the hot Australian sun. Not a bad holiday by anyone's standards, but definitely not the holiday Terry had imagined. And by now, Terry had had enough.

Every morning at dawn he'd woken to check

the surf, optimistically hoping the weather had changed overnight and that Huey, the god of surf, had sent some swell. Every morning, he returned with only disappointment. And now, on their final morning, with the prayers to Huey dutifully said the night before, Terry woke early and, full of irrepressible optimism, left the campsite to check the surf.

"Our last day and still barely a ripple," he reported as he returned to the tent to deliver the morning surf report.

"That's nice, luv," replied Lorraine, still half asleep and unhappy that it was only half.

Lorraine had no interest in surfing and had made the most of the lazy days, sunbaking and reading on long, white stretches of beach with barely a soul in sight.

"Nice?" said an indignant Terry. "We've come all this way for nothing!"

"That's nice, luv," she repeated, rolling over and trying to go back to sleep.

Terry stewed in his disappointment for a while before boredom finally got the better of him.

"I'm going fishing. I'll be back in an hour."

"That's nice, luv."

Terry gathered his fishing gear and set off to the southern end of the beach and from there, out onto the headland. He found a quiet spot, threaded some bait on a hook, and threw it carelessly into the ocean. Thirty-five minutes later, at the depth of his depression, he felt a tug on the line.

Suddenly the disappointment of the trip vanished and all his attention focused on the rod.

"Take it, fish. Take it!"

As if rising to the challenge, the rod dipped violently. Terry leapt to his feet as the reel began to wail, line spooling off rapidly. He'd hooked something, and it was big. He lifted the rod, but the fish fought back. The reel screamed again as more line was drawn out. The fish tore away from the rock ledge, but Terry was not to be denied. He tightened the drag on the reel and leaned back into the fight. He reeled furiously as the struggle became a battle of wills.

Suddenly the fish leapt out of the water, its long flank flashing in the sun.

"Holy Moses!" cried Terry, astonished by its size.

He kept the line tight as the fish rallied against him, running farther and farther out to sea in long, zigzagging arcs. Terry looked down and cursed himself for not keeping the reel in better condition as the last few thin strands of line threatened to run off the spool.

"Oh, come on!" he shouted, anticipating the end of the line. He tightened the drag further and prayed the line wouldn't break. Slowly, he began to reel the fish back in as more and more line found its way back on the reel.

Terry could sense the fish tiring. Fearing he would lose the fish at the last moment, he stepped down to the water's edge as he continued to haul the fish in.

Suddenly, the fish flashed in front of him, the silver of its scales gleaming in the sunlight. It was a big mulloway, almost a metre long.

Sensing the end, the fish lashed out with one final surge, but it was too late. Terry grabbed the fish behind the gills and hurled the fish, rod and reel up onto the rocks in one desperate motion.

The fish thrashed against the rocks, trying to flip itself back into the water, but Terry was on him like a shot. He scurried up to the fish, pinned it to the rocks, then dragged it to his knife.

The fight was over.

Terry sat back, staring at the fish, adrenaline still coursing through him. He hadn't expected to catch anything, let alone the brother of Moby Dick.

"Wait until Lorraine sees this!" he thought.

He quickly gutted the fish, packed up his fishing gear, and with the rod in one hand and his prize in the other, hastily trotted back to the campsite.

* * *

"Where are you going to put that?" Lorraine asked, astonished by the size of the fish.

"I thought we could eat it."

"It's huge!" she cried. "And we're going home today. How on earth are we going to cook it? I've already packed up all the pans."

"I don't know," Terry replied. "Maybe we should just take it home with us. There's enough to feed a family, maybe even two nights' worth. I'll see if I can whack it in the esky."

Terry soon discovered the fish was easily twice the size of the esky. There was only one thing to do. As much as he hated the thought of diminishing his prize, he cut the fish in half. After emptying almost everything else out of the esky, he finally managed to squeeze the fish inside.

"Rainey, be a luv and go get some ice, will you? I'll pack up the tent while you're gone."

Terry busied himself with the tent while Lorraine walked down to the service station and bought two bags of ice. By the time she returned, she was cranky. It had been a long, hot walk, and the ice was heavy.

"Why couldn't we have just picked up the ice on the way out?" she asked.

"I didn't think of that. Can you pour it into the esky while I finish up with the tent?"

Lorraine filled the esky while Terry finished packing up the campsite. He loaded the tent into the back of the car, then he and Lorraine lifted the esky into the boot.

"That fish is a monster! It's easily the biggest fish I've ever caught."

"Can we just go?" asked Lorraine. "We've got a long drive ahead of us and I'm already cranky."

"No worries. Why don't you just sit in the car? I'll go and square up with Rex."

Terry raced off to settle the bill for the campsite, unwittingly leaving the boot wide open.

"Did you see the size of that fish?" Bongo asked Horatio.

"Yes. That was a big fish."

"And you're hungry, right?"

"I'm starving."

"Well, what are we waiting for?"

Bongo dashed out of the bushes and made a beeline for the car.

"What the?" said Horatio. "Wait for me!"

He raced after Bongo, who in an instant had leapt onto a picnic table, run along the top, and jumped into the boot of the Fairlane. Horatio followed immediately behind.

Lorraine felt the two bumps in the back of the car, but dismissed them as Terry's careless packing settling into place and went back to reading her book.

"All sorted," Terry said as he returned to the car, noticing the open boot. "I thought I shut that." Without looking back, he gave the boot a good shove from the side, slamming it shut.

"The cave door has closed! We're trapped!" cried Horatio.

"Never mind that," Bongo said, already playing with the esky. "How do we get the fish?"

"I think I saw him push this and pull that," said Horatio, and the top of the esky popped open, revealing the rich aroma of the prize mulloway.

"Pay dirt!" cried Bongo. "Do you want the head or the tail?"

"Let's not do that again, please," replied Horatio.

"Just trying to be fair. I'll take the head."

The devils tore into the fish until there was nothing left but a few stiff fins.

"Oh man, that was good."

"I'll say," Horatio agreed. "Where do you think we are?"

"No idea, but it feels like we're moving. It feels a bit like when we were in that box on the way to the ooze."

"The zoo."

"You can call it what you like. I know what it was."

"Well, there's not much we can do trapped in here like this. I think I might just lie down and sleep off that fish. Wake me if anything happens."

"Okay, sure."

With the fish in their bellies, the constant hum of the car in their ears, and soft blankets for beds, both devils quickly drifted off to sleep. Twelve hours later, neither devil stirred as Terry drove the Fairlane up the ramp and onto the ferry.

THE BEACH

"Regretting your decision to join us yet, Wiru?" Jake asked as the three wallabies fought their way through the thick bush along the side of the river.

"Not yet," she replied, hopping past him, but the going was tougher than she had expected.

"Maybe we should get to higher ground and try to see where this crazy river is going," Wally suggested. "We seem to be backtracking every time the river changes direction."

Despite the effort involved in climbing another hill, Jake and Wiru agreed. They had spent too much time fighting their way through the bush only to have to fight their way back when the river turned on itself.

At the top of the next hill, they could see the river's path meandering through the bush and quickly realised they could take a shortcut through open fields to the south and meet up with the river further east, rather than following every bend. Once they reached the open field, they made ground easily.

"This is more like it," Wally said as they sailed across the open ground.

By the time their path met the river again, the soil had changed. It was becoming soft and lighter coloured. The foliage was thinning too, with fewer tall trees. A short way from where they rejoined the river, it swung north again, and a small sandy hill rose before them, covered in strange plants Wally had never seen. They began to climb the dune, slipping backwards with each step on the soft, shifting sand.

As their heads cleared the top of the dune, the full magnitude of the ocean lay in front of them, glimmering in the sunshine, stunning them into silence. So much water. So impossibly huge.

Jake broke the silence with the obvious. "That's a lot of water."

"It sure is," replied Wally, barely able to believe his own eyes.

He wandered down the beach toward the water, almost doubting it was real, until the soft sand between his toes was washed away by the water lapping at his feet. He looked northward along the beach and saw the river emptying into the watery expanse. He knew then that they were finally there. This was the ocean.

He walked into the water until it was up to his shoulders, gentle waves lifting him as they passed, splashing his lips with its salty taste. He began to laugh as he stood there, a tiny, tiny speck in a vast blue sea.

* * *

The three wallabies lay on the beach in the late afternoon, tired but victorious. Wally stared at the clouds overhead, a thousand shapes and no shapes at all, moving slowly across the sky from the ocean to the land. The clouds carried the rain, but it wasn't until now, looking out to the horizon at the endless expanse of water, that he realised the clouds were born at the edge of the ocean.

He could see them making their long journey across the sky, high above the ocean, heading inland, where they would bring the rain that would turn the grass green.

And when the rain fell and the plants had enough to drink, the water that was left would run down in tiny streams, collecting in rivers just like the one they had followed. Eventually, the rivers carried the water back to the ocean, where it would wait once again to become a cloud. It was a perfect cycle.

Wally wondered what would happen if the cycle ever broke down or was damaged. Without water, the plants would wither and die, and the animals that fed on them would starve, like the wallabies in his old mob, waiting for the rain. So would the kangaroos, koalas, and wombats, and anything else that ate the plants. And without those animals, the dingoes would vanish just as quickly.

When Gus had said, 'Go to the ocean', Wally had thought the ocean was just a place. But it was more than that. It was the wheelhouse of life. He understood that now, and why Gus had thought it was so important for him to go there. The more he thought about it, the more he realised that everything was connected and in almost perfect balance.

"I can see a wombat", said Jake.

"Where?" asked Wiru.

"Up there," he said, pointing to a large, fluffy cloud.

"That looks more like an echidna to me," said Wiru. "See? You can see its quills."

Wally could see the echidna too, and although he knew it was just a cloud, it was more than that. The cloud carried the promise of life for the echidna. And the wombat. And everything else for that matter.

THE SPIRIT

When Lorraine went to retrieve a blanket from the boot of the Fairlane after it had emerged from the bowels of the ferry at the destination, nothing could have prepared her for the sight that was waiting to greet her. But when the boot popped open and revealed the uninvited passengers, she shared a moment with the devils, each of them wide eyed with surprise and frozen in shock. It was the last thing in the world she had expected to see, and she let everyone on the wharf know with an ear-piercing scream.

"Terry!" she cried. "There are devils in the boot!"

Bongo saw the opportunity and quickly turned to Horatio.

"The cave entrance has opened! Quick, Hozza, now's our chance!"

The devils scrambled over the ledge of the boot and bolted for the long grass by the side of the wharf.

"Rainey, are you alright?" Terry asked as he

raced around to the back of the car.

"No!" she wailed. "There were devils in the boot!"

Not knowing Lorraine for her spiritual beliefs, Terry had grave concerns that his girlfriend of two years was suddenly showing signs of religious hallucination.

"What on earth are you talking about?" he asked. "What devils?"

"They were in the boot!"

Terry looked at the chaos inside the boot, completely baffled by the scene.

"Hey," he said finally, "where's my fish?"

The devils ran through the thin grass on the side of the harbour, trying to find somewhere to hide. Fortunately, they had arrived late in the day, and the twilight provided some cover. They made their way along the waterline, darting into the grass where they could, when something caught Horatio's eye. He stopped abruptly, staring in disbelief.

It was a flower, and not just any flower.

Bongo tore past him and stopped.

"Hozza! We don't have time to smell the flowers!"

"Wait, Bongo. It's not just a flower." He cast his gaze back to the large boat, now resting peacefully in the harbour, a short distance from where they had run into the grass.

"The boat, Bongo. Look."

"Forget the boat! Let's go!"

"Read what's on the side of it!"

Bongo looked over and tried to read what was painted on the side of the boat, now lit up by the lights of the wharf.

"Spi..., Spirito..., Spiritoft..."

"Oh, for heaven's sake, Bongo! It's the Spirit of Tasmania! We're home!" said Horatio, scarcely able to believe his own words.

"What?" asked Bongo, stunned. "Home?"

"That flower. It's a Tasmanian Angel. They only grow in Tasmania, and that boat over there, that's the Spirit," said Horatio, still trying to come to terms with what he was seeing.

"You are a dead set genius, my friend. I don't know how you managed to figure it all out, but we're home!"

"We're home?" repeated Bongo, reeling from what Horatio was saying. "Wait. I'm a genius?"

"Yes, you are, you crazy, stupid genius! You've done it!" Horatio grabbed Bongo in a headlock and ruffled the fur on the back of his head.

"We're home!" he cried as the realisation finally sank in.

"Yes, I've seen that boat before. That's the

boat that sails into the great water." Bongo looked around at the harbour and the sea beyond, letting the fresh, cold wind blow across his face. Horatio was right, there was no doubt. They were home.

He sat down in the grass, staring out to the ocean. The journey was all but over. All they had to do now was find their families. He had no idea how he'd managed to get them home, and it didn't matter. The important thing was that he had done it.

Tears welled in his eyes again, just like they had at the lookout at the Divide.

"Are you alright?" Horatio asked.

"I'm having another moment. I'm going to warn you now, so just stay out of my face about it, alright?"

Horatio just laughed.

"You have all the moments you like."

HOME

The wallabies spent the night on the beach, lulled to sleep by the gentle lapping of the ocean against the sand. In the morning, they woke early, just as the sun rose over the horizon and treated them to their very first ocean sunrise. Wally hopped down to the water and looked out across the sea, still in awe of the size of it. He turned his gaze to where the ocean met the sand and watched the waves break on the shore. The beach was long and empty, perfect for a good, long hop.

"So where to now, chief?" Jake asked as he joined Wally at the water's edge.

"Down there, I'd say," Wally replied, pointing to the southern headland. "Looks pretty green to me, plenty of trees. Why don't we go and take a look?"

"Sounds good to me," said Wiru, already leading the way down the beach.

The wallabies travelled easily along the beach on the hard, wet sand at the edge of the water, splashing through the shallows as they went. The waves were larger than the day before, and they began to play with the water as it chased them up the beach. When they finally approached the headland, they saw that Wally's hunch had been right.

The headland stretched out from the land, as though trying to push its way into the great ocean, while waves broke around its base, relentlessly pushing it back. The very tip of the headland stood exposed, its stony cliffs pitted with caves and the rocky scars of an enduring battle with the elements. Closer to shore, the headland curved inward, forming a bay of tranquil water that lapped against a white, sandy beach. Trees and grasses surrounded the beach, offering both food and shade.

"This should keep us busy for a while," said Jake as the wallabies tried to take it all in. "Where do we start?"

"Maybe we should start with them," said Wally, finally noticing they weren't alone.

Four wallabies waited at the end of the beach, high up in the dunes. They would have seen the trio bounding along the beach, and it was now obvious the newcomers were being watched. Wally acknowledged them with a nod, and all four started to make their way down from the dunes toward them.

"You three aren't from around here, are you?" said the first of the wallabies as he approached.

"No, we're not. We've come in from the west, beyond the Divide," replied Wally.

"You've been travelling for a while, then. That's quite a long way."

"You know of the Divide?"

"Of course." He smiled at Wally's surprise. "You don't think you're the only ones searching for something better, do you?"

He looked over to Jake and Wiru.

"So how did you all end up here?"

"That, my friend, is a very long story," said Jake, beaming at another opportunity to tell the tale, "but I'd be glad to share it with you sometime."

"I'll look forward to that," the wallaby replied. "And maybe we can share a few of ours. We've got a whole mob full of stories. You won't believe what some of us went through to get here."

"Oh, I think we have some idea," said Wally, smiling.

"Well, how about we show you around later and introduce you to our mob? It's not that big, but everyone's pretty relaxed. I'm sure you'll fit in, if that's what you're looking for."

"I'd like that," said Wally.

"Okay, great. But in the meantime, we're heading over to the south side of the headland. Why don't you come with us? The swell is just

starting to pick up and the inside peak is breaking.
Do you surf?"

The End.

If you enjoyed this book, please consider writing a review on the site where you purchased the book. It may help spread the word about the state of the wallaby populations in Australia and raise awareness of the increasing and alarming rate of animal extinction on the planet.

Every voice counts.

For more information about the book,
including the animals that feature in the book,
please visit:

www.thewobblywallaby.com